THE CONDITION IMPERVIOUS

BY CEON

Matador
Unit E2 Airfield Business Park,
Harrison Road, Market Harborough,
Leicestershire. LE16 7UL
Tel: 0116 2792299
Email: books@troubador.co.uk
Web: www.troubador.co.uk/matador
Twitter: @matadorbooks

ISBN 978 1800465 473

British Library Cataloguing in Publication Data.
A catalogue record for this book is available from the British Library.

Printed and bound in Great Britain by 4edge Limited
Typeset in 11pt Minion Pro by Troubador Publishing Ltd, Leicester, UK

Matador is an imprint of Troubador Publishing Ltd

This book is dedicated to my dear friend Hebe Dyson,
without whom I would not be here today.
Much love,
CEON

ACKNOWLEDGEMENTS

Thanks to Catherine Wills and Daniel Pike for listening to my endless updates on my progress of writing this.

Thank you to my friends: Finn Robinson, Hebe Dyson, Matthew Watson and Peter Walmsley for always being there for me.

Thank you to Clare Louise Roberts, Russ Withey and Chelsie Nash for always supporting and actively promoting me to follow my creative desires.

Special thanks to Elinor Prescott for lending her artistic skills for the cover art and to new friendships with herself and Katie Caparros-Midwood.

ONE

I used to love driving the river bend; the road was so close to the sand and water – I used to look out and imagine I was driving along the beach without the consequence of getting sand in and all over my car, let alone crushing anything that might be living on the sand. You didn't really need to watch the road as there was never anyone in sight until you hit the main roads again.

Today wasn't one of the days I could imagine, though; the clouds were grey and ready to burst, which perfectly reflected how I was feeling inside. Instead of staring outside, I stared at my hands on the wheel, in particular the wedding ring on my finger. I was driving back from the hospital where my wife Shannon had spent the last three months. Today felt different – she's never been worried through the months, but today I could tell there was something that wasn't sitting right with her. When I asked, she shrugged it off.

From driving in my haze, I woke up parked on top of Necksend cliff, which overlooks the sea of which the river by the road leads into. The rain was pouring down now. The song 'You Said' by False Advertising was playing loudly; I turned it down. The clock said it was 10:45am; I had lost around fifteen minutes of time. I don't understand how I got here without noticing; it's not a very welcome area for cars. Usually when I get stressed or anxious, I tend to doze off but only for a minute at most.

I got the car into gear and prepared to reverse the way I came. Things like this didn't usually happen; I had never blacked out before. I would probably be shocked if I hadn't been so emotionally drained by everything happening to my wife. But right now, I was just numb.

I started reversing the car. *Thud.* It instantly rolled over something, and when the back tyre hit the ground, I lost all control of the car; it started skidding, leading the tail towards where the car was facing before but not stopping. The rain had turned the mud into a dark flume.

I tried to turn the wheels in the opposite direction and accelerate, but it made it slide more; my hands slipped off the wheel, one knocking the volume up.

I decided I should jump out, but before I could unfasten my belt, the wheels were off the ground and in the air. The car nosedived first, straight towards the water like a professional diver. Everything happened so quickly; I didn't want to see where I was headed so instead stared out the rear and watched a fountain of sludge follow the car to the sea.

The car hitting the water made a slapping sound and thrust me forwards, hurting my neck on the belt and my feet against the bottom of the dashboard. The belt pulled me back as the car started to sink. I tried opening the door but the water against it was too strong. Water started pouring in from each seal on the doors. The water was usually misty brown but, because of the mess my car made, the watered-down mud made it a much darker chocolatey colour.

I unfastened my seat belt and my torso fell straight into the wheel, which only made the car start to sink quicker. I looked around, trying to figure out what to do while the water poured in. Scrambling around trying to think, I paused to calm down my breathing and to think. The window! I tried the button, but the electric was fried. I put both hands on the head of the seat and started swinging my legs into the window, I think the crash into the water had dislocated my left ankle. I held my breath each time I kicked and let out a yell at every landing. It didn't seem to be doing anything other than putting my body through worse pain. The water was up to my chin by this point. I decided to stop and take my final breaths before being submerged in water.

When the water filled the car, all I could hear was the ricketing of water. It was an oddly peaceful setting for something that'd surely kill me. Maybe if I lost my life now, Shannon would be spared; the world needs her much more than it'd ever need me. I gave up and tried to stay calm with the thought that Shannon may be spared, a life for a life. It started with my body begging for air so much that I couldn't hold it in any longer and let my body gag for air, taking in the mucky water; naturally, my body tried to spit it back out, which just made re-inhaling it all the worse – my eyes started to throb, my ears experienced cramping pains and a sharp ring, as if I had just been to a gig. My throat started to close up, causing me to hold my breath without my control. I thought I'd be able to feel the water in my lungs, but I just felt inside how I felt on the outside. I was weightless. I could feel all these different pains, but it was still calm. The car was still sinking. My throat felt like it was being crushed by someone grabbing it tighter and tighter, until it couldn't get any smaller anymore. My eyes started to close, causing me to lose even more control of my body – this was it.

Darkness.

*

I was startled awake. The shock through my body caused me to launch forwards and gasp for air; much to my further surprise, I swallowed another gulp of water. I opened my eyes and saw my surroundings were the same apart from the car, which was now at the bottom of the waterbed. Did I not die? If I had passed out, surely, I would've taken in even more water? Whereas now, I felt airier, bar the water I had just swallowed upon waking. My ears were no longer ringing nor did my eyes sting; my leg was no longer dislocated. I thought to myself, *right, this is a sign to fight.* I got up and started kicking the window again. I kicked and kicked and kicked, nothing. I changed plan and started with my shoulder, trying with all my will to break the window, but. it. wasn't. budging. In my frustration, I started to let out a scream; no sound came out of my mouth, only bubbles. As a result of my scream, I inhaled too much water and again, my eyes hurt, ears became shell-shocked. I started trying with my shoulder again, this time whacking my head on the roof.

Black.

*

Again, I jump started awake, gulping in the now misty brown water. I started to freak out, more and more questions flew round my mind at high speed. My heart pounded in my chest. I couldn't breathe. I was having a panic attack. Great. My body paniced and gasped for air while I was engulfed in water. The sharp pains and sounds came even quicker this time and I tried to rest my eyes when my body couldn't scream anymore.

Blank.

*

Instantly, I grabbed on to my nose and held my breath, which made my chest puff out. I opened my eyes and here I was again. Maybe I had died and this was the afterlife: reliving my death over and over – *no*. I would not do this for the rest of time. I thought and thought and thought. What could I use to break the window? My coffee flask? The cigarette lighter? I got it! The bottom of the headrest! I took out the headrest and I rammed it into the window, using all of my body weight to put pressure onto it and, eventually, after a minute or so, the window shattered. I grabbed on to the outer of the door and propelled myself through the window and started swimming upwards. I couldn't really see much through the misty waters, but I swam knowing there would be air at the top, freedom from this nightmare. I was pushing so hard to swim. My throat started to crush into a pinch, eyes throbbing, ears screaming, eyes closing, not again, not now, please no.

Shadows.

*

This time, being jolted awake caused me to swallow granules. I opened my eyes and the granules hit them, too. I flipped my body over; I had woken up face first on the sea floor, swallowing sand and the likes – I looked around and my car wasn't in sight. This time, I kicked off the ground and started frantically swimming upwards. I wish I could say I swam elegantly like a mermaid or a diver, but instead I was more like a cat that had fallen into the bath, desperate to jump out at the top. I was so determined; I was not going to pass out again.

I got to the point where I could see light shining through the muck; I pushed even harder until I popped out of the top, taking a huge breath, taking all the air I could.

The day had changed, no more rain or grey clouds but a bunch of white, fluffy clouds, with the sun peering out from behind them. I couldn't believe how much the weather had changed since earlier; it was as if it was a whole other day.

I looked around and spotted the shore in the distance. My body was so stressed out and tired, it just wanted to stop, but it was only one last swim to get to land. As I was swimming, I was trying not to think about whatever had just happened but instead worry about getting home. I remembered visiting this beach when me and Shan first moved here; she went out on her paddle board and I stayed on the beach reading a book – she wouldn't believe how much I had swum today. When she came back in with her board, I went to pretend to help her and instead wrestled her in the water; we were giggling so much, one of many treasured memories with her. Thinking back made the swim go quicker; when I reached the beach, I remembered there was a bus stop opposite the car park. My wallet was still in my pocket, although I was dripping wet so I could only imagine what state my cash was in. I had no way of telling when the next bus was going to be; the bus shelter was old and the windows were smashed up, so there were none of the new additions like a digital clock. So, I sat and waited. Shivering the whole wait.

When the bus came, I hopped on and tried to order a ticket into town, but nothing came out right; I was slurring as if I had been drinking all day. The driver asked for the money and held out her hand; I took out my wallet and a puddle of water dripped out of it – she gave me a judgemental look over her glasses, which were at the end of her nose, and yanked her hand away.

"Just get on," she huffed and rolled her eyes.

Although I am Scottish myself, since moving back here, I'd found it hard to read fellow Scots; at times, they could seem rude, but really they were just direct. Certainly, this woman was judging me, but even through her judgement, she showed me kindness; she could've easily rejected my wet money and left me by the side of the road to fend for myself.

Luckily, the town we lived in was only small, so I was able to walk from the bus stop back home. When I got in, I threw my keys in the dish and instantly turned the heating on and changed into fresh clothes. I was still shivering and in a delusional state of sleepiness. I wondered how much time it had been since visiting Shan this morning and this whole ordeal that I had just been through. I wrapped a blanket around myself and went to find my phone (which I thankfully left at home today). I had missed fourteen calls, some from work, some from the hospital and some from Shan's family. I looked at the time and it was 1:30pm, three and a half hours after I had left the hospital. I started to feel short of breath; still shivering, I sat down wrapped in my blanket. I couldn't believe I had missed so many calls in such a short space of time. I hoped Shan was alright. Struggling to keep my eyes open, I looked at my phone again to start calling people back and I noticed something strange: it said that today was Thursday, which couldn't possibly be right because today is Monday; then I looked at the calls and they were missed days ago. *What?* How could three days have passed? My brain was fried; I must just be confused? Maybe I just forgot what day it was. My eyes closed again and my breathing stopped.

*

When I woke up, I was thrust forwards and gasped – it was 1:30pm on Friday. This made no sense – what was happening? My shivering had stopped, my breathing normal and I felt well-rested and clear of mind. With more missed calls, I didn't hesitate to grab Shan's keys and drive straight to visit her; if I had really been away for four days, then she must feel so alone and abandoned by me – I felt awful. I put my hands on the wheel and they instantly started shaking; flashes of the incident flew through my mind – I shook my head. No, I needed to go see her.

TWO

When I got to the hospital, I flew past the reception and speed walked towards her wing. When I was in the corridor, I was stopped.

"Oh, Mrs Dyson, what are you doing here?" Doctor Long was clutching a clipboard and was wearing a bright purple button-up shirt under her jacket.

"I'm coming to visit Shan."

She raised her eyebrows and put her hand on my shoulder. "The receptionist had some trouble getting hold of you; the family said they would speak to you, eh." She let out a deep breath. "I'm so sorry, but Shannon passed away on Monday at around 11am."

Everything stopped working, starting with my ears replaying the exact sounds I heard underwater; my eyes started to blur, my mouth was moving but only letting out noises. "Pff, grrg, uhuh*uh*." My legs gave up and I fell to the ground, tears streaming from my eyes as I clutched my chest, feeling like my heart had exploded. Shannon was my life; we had spent our whole lives together – she couldn't die; she couldn't be *dead*. What was I supposed to do without her? Who was I supposed to be? I let out a huge wail which made everyone in the corridor stop and look at me. I felt like I couldn't breathe.

The doctor crouched down and put her hand on my back. "Come on, you can sit in my office, and I'll get you a coffee." She led me to her office and popped out to get a coffee. I sat there and stared at the open window; it was a few floors up – I thought of how easy it'd be for me to jump out and join Shan, wherever she was, but I also knew that wouldn't be what she wanted.

Doctor Long came back with a machine-made black coffee and put her hand on my shoulder as she placed it in front of me. "You can sit here as long as you need; I'll come see you again in ten minutes."

I quickly drank the coffee and sat sniffling before leaving after five minutes. I needed fresh air. I left the hospital and drove out towards the hills. I parked in the first space I could find and ran out in the fields. I screamed, cried, ran around and curled up in a ball on the ground, remembering my whole life with Shan.

*

I don't remember how we met; it was so long ago – her parents said we came out of nursery one day holding hands and were glued at the hip since.

I think we both realised we were gay around the same time. We were so open with each other that we would've told each other straight away if we each didn't as quickly realise we were each in love with the other.

She was always the brave one, so after three years of us

both knowing we were gay (we were around sixteen at the time), she told me first. She came over to my house and as soon as she came into the room, she sheepishly sat at the end of my bed, which wasn't like her, as she was usually full of life. "OK, I need to get this out the way," she said, tapping her thighs and looking down.

I crawled to the bottom of the bed and held her hands. "You can tell me anything."

She let go of my hands and looked at me with her beautiful brown eyes. "If you're uncomfortable or need time to process, you can always ask me to leave."

I started to feel worried for her and my face must've reflected that.

"OK." She took a deep breath and ran her hand through her hair. "I am gay and I'm in love with you."

I was shocked; I really couldn't believe that the woman I had loved most of my life (without always knowing) loved me back. I thought it was maybe a trick and she had realised my secret and was trying to prompt me to come out, but I knew her better than that and knew she would never do anything like that.

When I woke from my daze of thoughts, she was staring at me, worried, trying to read my reaction, her eyes welling up with tears. I grabbed her face and pulled her close to me and kissed her. Three years in fear for nothing.

After a few months together, she asked if she could start telling people at school, which was terrifying, but I didn't care; the only thing I cared about was her – it's not like it'd affect my social status; my only friends were Shan and a guy called Johnny. We never sat together because Shan was very popular and she didn't get along with Johnny very well; she said he made her uncomfortable and was adamant that he fancied me, which I had never seen. One day at lunch, she walked to mine and Johnny's table, grabbed my hand and stood on top of a table as I stood on the ground next to her. Everyone stopped what they were doing and stared at her.

"Ahem." She cleared her throat to get everyone's attention. "I just wanted to say that I'm gay and very in love with my beautiful girlfriend Eden." She gestured towards me on the ground. "That's all, thanks." Her female friends all crowded round her and said how brave she was and that they were happy that she was happy; I sat back down with Johnny, who didn't say anything, but I think he just didn't know what he was supposed to say. I saw those girls in the corridor later in the day and they again said they were happy for Shan but questioned why she was with 'such a loser'. Shannon had a day filled with girls saying she was brave and guys saying 'that's hot'. Everyone loved her – it was impossible not to. After school, when I was waiting to walk back with Johnny, I got beat up by a group of guys, probably jealous that they couldn't be with Shannon, calling me a 'faggot' and telling me I was nothing. They left me lying on the ground and Johnny peeled me off the floor when he arrived.

Shannon was angry when she found out how I got my black eye and sore ribs, but as much as she wanted to do something about it, I asked her not to. She insisted on me sitting with her and her friends on lunches because she felt she needed to protect me, but I felt much more comfortable sitting with Johnny than her friends who hated me.

A few years after high school, Johnny and I stopped seeing each other as he started his own business and moved further into England, around the same time that we moved to Scotland. We still spoke sometimes but generally, we were too busy.

*

I woke from my reliving of memories still curled up on the field; it was starting to get dark, so I got up to walk to the car park. I ended up having run around forty minutes away from my car. It was getting darker but keeping grey for now. I got to the top of a hill that was overlooking the car park at the other side of the road. I could hear a car revving in the distance. I got over the hill to face the car park behind a road bend.

I looked both ways and nothing was coming. I walked over one side of the road and saw a red flash speed round the corner towards me and, before I could act accordingly, it hit me, whacking my left hip off the bonnet first. The car was going so fast it flipped me over the roof doing somersaults, my left leg flopping around lifeless and as if it had no bones. I saw the ground racing towards me, black tar and yellow lines all blurred together. The bottom of my left jaw hit the ground first, making a haunting crunching sound.

Darkness again.

*

When I came to and took my breath, I heard a cracking noise from my nose rubbing against the ground and felt my face scraping against dirt. I pushed myself up as you would in a push up. I was now in the long grass next to the car park. The people that hit me probably hid my body and drove away, arseholes. I stood on my left leg perfectly fine. I looked around and noticed walkers staring at me, an older couple who were obviously concerned about what I had been doing face first in the grass. I gave them a wave and they ducked their heads, quickly moving along, clearly put off by me.

I got into Shannon's car, sat and took a deep breath. I looked at the dashboard; it was now Saturday morning.

I tried to think about and make sense of what happened; the crunching sound played in circles in my mind, making me remember the pain, which made me need to open the door and vomit.

I think I had died. I think I had died every time. There was only one way to find out.

THREE

I needed to kill myself, but how? Such an insane thought, considering that I had died six times and the only way to prove it was true was to die a seventh. Maybe I was in a coma and dreaming up all of this mad shit. Maybe I did die the first time, and this was what the afterlife was. I was so gifted to have spent over twenty years with Shannon in my life; maybe this was my punishment for not being worthy. For never becoming worthy. Maybe I held her back from becoming even more spectacular than she was. I loved her so much. I would always love her.

I decided that on this wild conclusion, I must sleep before I did anything rash, so I began to drive home.

I had to drive via the river bend. As soon as the car hit the road, my hands started shaking and it became difficult to breathe – I tried to focus on the end of the road and started driving a bit faster, over the limit; the quicker I was off the road, the sooner these feelings would evaporate. I started to hear the water stuck in my ears again and in a blink, the car filled with water. I slammed my foot on the brake and the car skidded a little; I instantly jumped out, expecting to be drenched in water, but I was bone dry. I vomited in the middle of the road. "My apologies to whoever drives through that."

I looked back at the car and there was nothing in it. Maybe I was just triggered. Obviously, it wasn't real, even if it felt like it was. I got back into the car and my body continued to shake and my ears filled with water, but I closed my eyes until car horns cut through and they were rid of the water. I had made it to the turning into the motorway. I had to quickly open the door and vomit again, the seat belt tugging me backwards into the car. "Ugh, gross."

I managed to get as far as locking the front door before crumbling to the ground in tears; I couldn't live here alone – this was *our* home. I cried myself to sleep face first on the floor just before the stairs.

I could hear shifting and clanking and felt something heavy on my chest. I opened my eyes, and it was pitch black apart from a few stars looking down on me. I couldn't see much at all but could feel from my surroundings that I was in some sort of ditch. I sat myself upwards and could now see shadows of trees and the silhouettes of two women, each with one arm out towards me. I couldn't make out any of their features; everything was just black. I stood up and realised my ditch was more of a pit. Looking up at the arms again, I noticed one was holding a huge knife and the other was holding a syringe. Behind them flashed the colours green and purple; the flashes hurt my eyes so I looked away to the ground, gradually moving up to look around the pit. I noticed a message written in stones on the dirt wall: 'Choose correctly'. I turned to look at the arms again and they quickly swiped away, instead being replaced by a huge wave of water but not normal water – it was jet black, more like tar but still the consistency of water, of which its only direction was straight into me. 'You Said' started playing loudly out of the sky with the stars flashing to the beat; I braced myself for the hit of water.

I woke up in a pool of sweat still face first on the floor; it was just a nightmare this time. That was slightly more explainable than any other events recently, so I took that as a win for sanity.

I stood up and walked up the stairs to go to bed, tripping up the top step and falling into the wall in front of me. I took off all my clothes and dived face first into bed, instantly falling asleep when my face hit the pillow.

This time, I was awoken by knocking on the door. I had been drooling on the pillow, my hair was everywhere and I absolutely *reeked*. Having to quickly grab my clothes off the floor to throw on just added to the mess that I was. I opened the door to Shan's parents; her mum instantly pouted when taking a look at me and pounced on me with a hug, crying in my ear and not letting go, pushing me further into the house, her dad following and closing the door behind him. He cleared his throat and put his hand on his wife's shoulder. She raised her head and looked at me while daintily wiping tears off her face with her index finger. They both walked into the living room and sat on the sofa.

"Tea?"

They both nodded.

While waiting for the kettle to boil, I splashed my face with cold water in an attempt to look a bit cleaner. I struggled to catch my breath, my head spiralling towards that day on Necksend. I was interrupted by Steve (Shan's dad) clearing his throat and holding on to the door frame at the other side of the room. "The kettle."

I raised my head, water dripping from my face onto my shirt, my hands firmly gripped across the edge of the counter and the inside of the sink. I looked over at him and he nodded towards the kettle, making one of the hairs on his styled cut fall out of place. He looked tired; they both did. The bags under his eyes made it look like he hadn't slept in months, which was probably about right.

I took their teas and they both sat cupping the mugs on their laps, staring into their tea like it was going to put on an unmissable showing. We sat in silence for what felt like hours. No one even daring to breathe deeper than needed, to not make a sound, as if we'd all fall apart if the slightest noise was made. We were all so fragile; a huge part of our lives had disappeared – I wondered if they had started losing their sanity too but decided to keep my experiences to myself.

I looked at them – Shannon looked nothing like either of them; she was completely perfect. Her parents had always been so kind to me, especially when my own weren't. They always made me feel welcome and Shannon wasn't scared to be affectionate when they were around.

I couldn't stand the silence; my ears filled with a mixture of the noise of the water and the song that was playing at the top of Necksend – I needed to block it out; I needed to make noise before I screamed and had a meltdown.

I looked up at them again; it was dark outside now. I cleared my throat. "She left a USB."

They both looked up at me, a bit shocked that the silence had been broken.

"A-a video of what she wanted if she…" I took a gulp. "Passed."

They both nodded and I went upstairs to get it, plugging it into the TV when I arrived in the living room again.

As soon as Shannon's face appeared on the screen, her mum started wailing. Her dad sat with his head between his arms and his hands through his previously groomed hair. I started to feel stabbing pains in my chest, and I clutched on to it, tears flowing through my eyes.

The video consisted of her explaining what she wanted from her funeral and who she wanted to have which of her belongings. She must've filmed this when she first found out she was sick; she still looked healthy and full of life – she waited until she had been in hospital for a month to give me the USB. She finished the video by stating how much she loved us all and how she hoped we wouldn't dwell on her passing and try to live happy and full lives. In reality, my life would never be whole again without her, and I could tell it was the same case for her parents.

We had a funeral to sort and attend; I couldn't go through with my plan until I had let people say goodbye to the best woman this world had ever seen, and I needed to say a proper goodbye, too.

I offered to let her parents stay while we went through everything, but they insisted that they couldn't be around her belongings and old home for that long.

FOUR

Photo albums sprawled across the floor, golden light shining through a crack in the blinds, I sat staring at the pictures of her but not seeing them at all. My mind was blank and everything was numb. I was startled awake from my daze by my own deep breathing as one single tear slid down my left cheek.

I slowly began to curl up on the floor, one arm under my head, the other cradled between my legs. I imagined Shannon there spooning me, even though that was my job when she was here.

I could hear a whooshing sound gradually get louder and louder from outside; I tried to ignore it but it got so loud that I had to get up and look out the window. Somehow, the golden light had disappeared without me noticing. It was now raining, but the drops on my window were black, leaving streaks behind their path. I looked around and couldn't find where the whooshing was coming from. I closed my eyes and listened as it got louder and louder. I looked to the right, and there it was coming round the corner, smacking into one of the houses on its way round, making a slapping sound: a huge wave of water. This time, it wasn't black but instead was mucky. I could see something floating near the top but couldn't make out what. The wave came down the road and took a big turnaround at the house directly across from mine and faced me. The wave grew higher and higher; I could now just see what was floating in the middle of the wave: it was me. Unconscious and with no control over my limbs, I just stared at it in shock – how could that be me?

The wave began to crash down; I braced myself for whatever kind of impact it'd cause.

My phone started ringing and the glare took my eyes' attention away from the window for the slightest second. Looking back out the window, the wave had gone, as had my body, and the windows were clean with no black streaks.

The phone stopped ringing and I received a text within seconds; it was Shannon's mum, Sheila.

'Just calling to check if you needed anything for tomorrow, even if it's just someone to talk to, you'll always be part of our family xoxo'

It was the funeral tomorrow. The three of us had planned it together, hoping to have made it the way Shannon would've wanted and to give everyone a fair chance to say goodbye. When Shannon died, a huge part of me died, too. I didn't think I'd ever accept that she was gone, nor would I come to feel whole again. Look at me – before I even knew she had died, I started losing my mind, I think; I didn't know how else to explain these strange experiences. I felt like they definitely happened: the sounds, the feelings, the visuals were all too real, but they were all unexplainable, and why hadn't anyone else witnessed or questioned such things? I still needed to follow through with my theory but after the funeral. The worst thing that could happen was that I actually died, but then that'd mean I wouldn't need to live with the pain of being without Shannon, so it wasn't that much of a loss for me. My work would easily replace me; the area manager and my assistant manager had been doing a great job of watching the bank the last few months while I'd been off on leave. They gave me a very generous furlough when Shannon got sick, not earning as much money as usual but having all the time in the world to be with and look after her – they really look after their staff's personal needs. I wouldn't be hurting anyone either; Shannon was all I really needed so I never stepped out of that bubble.

I wasn't sure what I'd do if I survived; I wouldn't know what the right action to take would be – should I walk into an asylum? Should I consult a doctor? My thoughts kept racing through my mind, so fast that I couldn't follow them all and ended up switching off to everything happening around me.

I decided that when I was going to do it, I'd jump off of the building Shannon rented her dance space in; it was closed on Wednesdays so no one would see and I would be able to use her key to get in. That gave me two days to mentally prepare and to back out if I wasn't sure, which I wasn't totally convinced, but I needed answers.

It wasn't right that this was taking up so much space in my mind when Shannon had just passed, and I hated myself for it. I should be mourning, but maybe this was my mind's reaction and my own strange way of dealing with it, but if that were true, then my mind would be tricking me into ending my life, and I knew that would disappoint Shannon, something I'd never intentionally do.

FIVE

Steve, Sheila and I stood in a line at the front of the church. People consoled us, shook our hands, touched our shoulders, hugged and even cried in our arms. Even Shannon's friends, who'd never liked me, gave me hugs and expressed how much they missed her and told me how strong I was. Shannon never noticed that they weren't keen; she tried to see the best in people and it would've really upset her if she'd known what they thought. I bet she'd be happy to see them being kind towards me.

Getting up and saying my goodbye in front of everybody felt like someone had grabbed my heart and was gripping on to it, waiting for it to crumble. I would've cried if I hadn't cried so much beforehand. I was glad I didn't, though; too much moisture had been making me black out and fall straight back into the sea, completely out of body but also physically there, feeling it all again.

We got out of the church and were all going to go to a bar for the reception. It was now raining, and people pulled out black umbrellas. I didn't see who, but someone handed me one; I opened it up and walked out of shelter; a gust of wind came and the rain changed to diagonal and soaked my face. My body started shaking, my neck craning from side to side; I could feel something run from my nose; I saw a drop of blood drip from my face, disparaging in the mud beneath me. I dropped the umbrella and my body started uncontrollably spasming, causing me to hit the ground flinching and shaking. I couldn't breathe; I felt submerged in water again. Not here. Not now. This was a day to honour Shannon's life – why did my body have to do this?!

I felt someone grab me, their arm around my stomach, and drag me into the back seat of a car. I kept flashing from people looking at me to being underwater.

When I finally came around, one of Shannon's male friends was looking at me, her parents in the background, sobbing. He brushed his shaved head with his hand. "Ye alright?" I wish I remembered his name. "Want me to drive you to the hospital?"

I shook my head; there was no chance I was ready to explain any of this to anyone – I didn't even understand it myself. "No, I'm OK, thank you." I stood up and a crowd of people stared at me. I heard some concerned mumbles and some disgusted grunts. I didn't care, though – why would I start caring what they thought now after all these years? I just didn't want to embarrass Shannon or take any light away from her day.

Not everyone that she knew was there, which I thought was odd but not completely strange; they would be able to say goodbye some other time in their own way. The rest of the night, everyone drank while I had water, which still made my chest feel weird while drinking it. Gradually getting drunker and louder, they shared their stories and photos of

Shannon, reminiscing about better days. She was always a light in everyone's lives.

Through the night, her friend Cassidy came over to me – she was naturally tanned and had black hair. She put her hand on my shoulder and looked deep into my eyes, her pupils growing bigger, pushing the green out the way. "I'm really sorry." She was very sincere, instantly ducking her head down and leaving the building. She seemed guilty. Obviously, Shannon's illness wasn't her fault.

SIX

All of Tuesday night, I couldn't sleep. I tossed and turned the whole time. When it finally hit 3am, I decided to get up; if I was going to do this then there would be no waiting around. I got dressed, never once looking in the mirror to see how I looked or to brush my hair.

I grabbed Shannon's studio and car keys. The drive, that was about thirty minutes, felt like it lasted two hours; I was continuously getting cold sweats and thoughts of *what the fuck are you doing* but, pushing through and choosing to ignore it, I couldn't live wondering anymore. This was too insane to not have answers.

I pulled into the empty car park, stopped and took a deep breath and closed my eyes. I could hear waves of water; I could feel splashes on my face – I shook my head to get away. I didn't know if it'd be worse being haunted by something that happened in my mind or being haunted by the fact that I seem to be indestructible.

My hands shook as I tried to put the key in the front door, struggling to fit it in and feeling sweat cover my forehead.

I decided to take the stairs to the top rather than the lift, most likely to stall and give myself more of a chance to think, even though my thoughts were a mix between *WTF* and *this might be my last ever walk.* Already having been sweaty with fear, I felt completely drenched at the end of the eight-flight walk and struggled to catch my breath; I was so unfit. The top door was a fire door; I hoped it wouldn't set off an alarm when I opened it, or maybe this was a sign to turn around and forget about this notion.

I clenched my fists and pressed the bar with my forearm, opening the door with no alarm raised. The wind was more powerful than it was on the ground, pushing my hair to cover my face, struggling to catch my breath, being constantly hit by wind. I walked slowly to the edge, closer to shuffling than walking, actually. I poked my head over, looking at the ground; I was facing the car park, not the best spot. I shuffled to the opposite edge: the back bin area – there were no cameras at the back, either, as there were no doors, so it wouldn't be on film, and if someone were to come along by chance, they'd be less likely to be at the back of the building. I once again closed my eyes and tried to take a deep breath; all I could hear this time was the wind, but my throat filled with water, causing me to choke up and vomit. I kneeled on the ground for a moment, trying to pull myself together. I pushed myself off the ground simultaneously with a large breath out. I planted my feet side by side on the roof, looking down at them for a moment. I let out a sigh, then looked up. Without thinking or giving my body a chance to react, I started sprinting towards the edge, hitting the rim and leaping off, no going back now.

The wind whistled in my ears, the concrete quickly moving towards me, my hair way behind my head; breathing was impossible without feeling like my lungs would fill up like a balloon and pop. As the ground approached, my automatic physical reaction was to cover my face.

My leg hit a large bin first, feeling like my whole leg had been ripped off my groin. I let out a scream which was cut short by the rest of my body hitting the ground, making a large whacking sound and multiple cracks coming from my body.

*

Then I woke up. Again. Gasping for air, I pushed my body off the ground and crawled so that my back was against a large, black bin, the one that caught my leg, I believe. There was loud chart music coming from the building, so it must've at least been a full day. I inspected my leg; nothing was wrong with it, no pain, no bumps and it moves perfectly. I raised my shaking hands to my face, feeling all around: no cracks, no bumps; in fact, my skin felt smoother than ever. I ran my hands through my hair and put my head between my knees, trying to gain control of my breathing again.

I raised my head and couldn't see anything through my eyes which were tearing up. "Fucking unkillable Eden Dyson." I sighed and punched the ground.

SEVEN

I quickly got up and ducked my head as I went to get into the car; I didn't want anyone seeing me. I walked across the car park, and although my eyes had stopped tearing up, my sight was still blurry and I felt weak, to the point of stumbling around. When I got into the car, I was breathing rapidly and was very clammy. I really needed some water. I grabbed a bottle that had been left in the glovebox and tried to quickly drink it, finding out it was warm at the wrong time and having to open the door to vomit. I felt super dizzy and started twitching, with my vision again flashing back and forth from being in the car underwater and being where I actually was.

I pulled down the mirror: I was as white as a ghost. In a blink, my reflection was myself underwater, even though I was here. I pushed down with force on the steering wheel, causing the horn of the car to wake me out of it. In doing so, I noticed that my knuckles had gone purple and were bleeding, throbbing from having hit the ground, and that the rest of my hand felt numb. I didn't notice before; I must've hit harder than I thought, but my brain was far too preoccupied to notice the pain.

Now that I'd called attention to myself via the horn, I needed to leave, even if I hadn't got myself together again yet.

All the way home, I was spaced out and I couldn't stop yawning; I struggled to grip the wheel because of how clammy I was. Luckily, I took the back roads and managed not to cause any accidents.

When I returned to Brigwiggs, I pulled the car into our driveway and finally had a chance to look at my phone – it was now Friday; how could two days have disappeared?! I couldn't keep losing days like this. I started back at work next week and I needed to turn up for my shifts. I wanted to wait until I got into the house to start trying to comprehend what was happening, but when I stepped out of the car, everything hit me at once: thoughts, memories, questions all flew through my head like a tornado and I started to feel dizzy again, so I ran. I ran so far out that I ended up on farming land, seeing visions of red flash on the road, feeling like I was falling with the wind hitting me as I ran; I really had no escape. I couldn't keep up with my thoughts; I couldn't make any sense or come up with a conclusion for what was happening to me. Was I born this way? Did someone do it to me? Were there others? Who should I tell? Who would believe me? What would they do to me? What should I do?

I got to the dead end of a road, panting and my body begging for water; my eyes were gradually covered by a static black until I was blinded with my eyes wide open. I fainted due to dehydration.

I woke around ten minutes later and walked home.

EIGHT

FIVE YEARS LATER.

I moved out of the house and into my own little flat in the middle of Brigwiggs, closer to the bank. That house was *our* dream home, but now that Shannon was gone, to me it was more of a nightmare, reminding me of what I had lost and what I had been through. I hadn't died since that day on the building five years ago, because how often did people really die accidentally? I decided not to tell anyone of the events after Shannon's death; I figured it'd bring nothing good. Steve and Sheila visited every week in the beginning but gradually came less and less; I figured it was too difficult for them. We rarely spoke at all now; I think we were all trying not to kill our lives with the past; I certainly was. I was trying to move forwards and forget about dying but, of course, always live with Shannon in my heart. I didn't get many flashbacks anymore, nor the strange dreams. I'd taken up running; it helped clear my mind, and also it was rather shocking how unfit I used to be. I mainly spent my days at work, home (reading) or running;

I didn't really partake in social events and preferred to keep to myself, apart from the yearly celebration of Shannon's life that her friends threw, even though they didn't speak to me. Sometimes, women asked me out or gave me their number at work, but that space in my heart would never be filled again. I'd saved up a lot of money in case of emergencies, especially with my 'condition'; I never knew what could happen.

There was yet another day that changed my life forever. I had followed my daily routine to a T as usual, jogging early in the morning, reading while walking to work and then working later than I needed to. When I was about to leave and go home, a few hours before closedown, a group of men wearing plastic lion masks and holding guns came in. One fired his shotgun at the ceiling and yelled, "Everybody get down – this is a robbery!"

Two men closed the front doors and another, who was holding an A-K type gun, added, "Comply, and no one gets hurt." One grabbed my shoulder and yanked me up, threatening to shoot the staff if I didn't fill their bags with money, which I was obedient to. Having filled their bags, the main one wanted me to escort them out of the building to ensure they weren't going to get trouble from the police.

While walking through the crowds, one was standing, staring down at a weeping woman; she was crying and whimpering rather loudly. His posture was tense, and I thought he was talking to her but I couldn't hear or see his lips. He sharply took a step back and raised his gun to point at her head but not touch it. "I'll tell you one more fucking time – stop crying, you bitch!" His voice cracked. His shouting made her start to wail louder and shiver. I started running towards them; if he was going to shoot her, I couldn't let it happen – I'd risk it and talk him down.

"That's it!" He was going to shoot her. I dived in front of the woman and heard the shot; my head felt a sharp burning and airy feeling. I didn't even feel myself hit the ground.

Black.

NINE

When I woke up with the usual gasp and lunge, my movement was restricted, and it was pitch black. Whatever was on top of me felt like rubber and restricted my airflow. I could hear a desk chair's wheels spinning.

"Holy…" they stammered. "Holy shit!" The wheels rolled again. "Eh-er-a-are you alive?" he asked sheepishly.

"Yes, could you please help?" The wheels rolled again but seemed headed away. I heard a short ripping noise, then, after a long pause, a zipping noise as my area became looser. I sat forwards and looked around. I was in a fucking morgue. There was a young lad with shaved black hair, just growing back from having been shaved, thick-rimmed black glasses and a white lab coat and scrubs staring at me in shock. He opened his mouth, but only small breaths were released. He slowly raised his arm towards me; he was holding a clear bag with what looked like my belongings. I took the bag. "Thank you very much." He slowly blinked and started steadily moving off the side of the seat, having fainted. I sat him up straight and put a cup of water from the fountain machine on the table next to him for when he woke up; I couldn't stay around to help him – maybe when he woke up he'd think it was a dream. Luckily, I still had all my clothes on and hadn't been pulled apart or whatever they do when you die.

I quickly ducked into the shop before leaving and bought a cap. It was navy blue and said 'I'm doing a great job'. I could hear the news loudly blaring from a TV in the cafe, which caught my attention.

"A Brigwiggs local, the manager of the bank, heroically dived in front of the bullet, saving the young woman's life but sadly, losing her own." It flashed to a picture of me with my name underneath. There's no way I could pretend that nothing had happened by continuing living in Brigwiggs, but now I didn't even think I could stay in the UK, depending how far the news had spread. A man with grey hair, that had a balding patch at the back, was sitting with his back to me, wrapped up in a dark green jacket and sipping his coffee. He had a pair of sunglasses sitting on the edge of the table that was closest to me. I couldn't believe that I was considering stealing, but I needed to do everything in my power to hide myself. I quickly snatched them and shuffled towards the exit. I half ran all the way home, trying to keep under as much cover as I could.

I got to my apartment, and nothing had been changed; no one had been inside. I let out a sigh of relief and checked my phone, learning that two days had passed. I quickly packed a bag of clothes and the money that I had saved and sped out of the place. Now, the tricky part was getting my car; it was parked in my rented spot in town.

I put a zip-up hoodie on and pulled the hood over my hat to try and leave me further unrecognisable. I walked past the bank, which was still closed. A shrine of flowers, candles and letters leant against the glass windows; I couldn't stop to look – I needed to keep going.

When I got to the parking building, I was sure to keep my head down so that no cameras could see me. My key card used to enter the building would surely cause alarm, but hopefully I'd be way out of town by then. When I started the car, the radio automatically turned on at the news.

"The woman's sacrifice meant that the robbers dropped everything and ran away, having this robbery turned into murder; they gave up on the money and didn't harm anyone else further."

I drove using mainly back roads. My plan was to make it as deep into England as I could, into a busy city and hopefully I'd get lost in the crowds of people. By the time I'd get there, the news cycle would've changed a good few times and no one would remember my face. I did consider going in the opposite direction, towards the highlands, to a quiet town or village like Baile Smachd or Airchall.

Around an hour into my journey, when I was near a place called Leafly, I saw blue lights flashing for me to pull over. "Shit, shit, shit." I gripped the wheel tighter as I pulled to the side. The officer came over to my car.

"I need to see your ID." He had blond eyebrows that were near invisible and his nose was so long I was surprised he could even see past it. "It says on our systems that the owner of this vehicle, Eden Dyson, is deceased," he said, scratching his head under his hat. He looked rather young but had heavy wrinkles under his eyes; I imagined he was new to the force and was stressed because it hadn't turned out how he thought it would. He stared me in the face.

"Well, I'm not sure what to say, sir – I am here and well." I nervously smiled. He let me go after inspecting my insurance for the car.

"I'll get that changed on the system for you so that you don't get further bother." He tapped the roof of the car while walking away.

I rolled up my window and started driving again. "*Fuck*," I said, slapping the wheel. Now people would know something wasn't right; I needed to get further out of view. I drove for a further fifteen minutes before pulling over the car and getting out to catch some air, calm down and come up with a plan. I was on a back road and didn't expect anyone to be around, so I pulled over and instantly ran out of the car. Unluckily for me, there was another car behind me that I failed to check for. I was instantly hit, the bonnet hitting my hip and taking out my leg, causing the rest of my body to land on top of it, whacking my head with a *crunch*.

TEN

When I came to, lunging forwards, I nearly hit the back of my car. I was now on the side of the road behind my car, the other car nowhere to be seen. It was dark now; I wondered if it had been two days again. I walked around to get into the front seat and there was a man sitting on my bonnet with his head in his hands. I cleared my throat. "Excuse me."

He slowly turned his head around, almost like an owl would. Reaching my direction, he jumped back and fell off the car. He was wearing a dark, puffy, sleeveless jacket and a white T-shirt advertising Dockeray beer. He picked himself up, using my car to lean on, and dusted off his clothes. "Are-are ye OK, pal?" His eyes widened. "Yer head was proper caved in, you ken? Mah burd has driven aff tae git help." He gestured up the road.

I shook my head and used my hands to touch it. "See, I'm alright, thanks, just need to get going." He moved to the side and got his phone out, most likely to phone his partner, his eyes never straying from my car.

I checked the time and date; it had only been an hour – usually, it lasts two days. Why was it quicker this time? I thought back to when I first drowned and remembered that I had died four times but came back three days later. I thought back to the red flash in the hills. I figured that if I had died a certain way before, that it takes less time for me to recover, not that I was trying to say there was any sense in these things that happened to me.

I drove further but struggled using the back roads in the pitch dark. It was nearing 10pm, and I was around two hours away from the border, when I saw a B & B advertised, 'The Shawnie family invites you'. The entrance led up a narrow dirt track that went on for around ten minutes. I pulled up at a large farmhouse. The downstairs lights were still on. When I turned off my engine, a couple were standing outside the house; they must've only been around their early fifties. I got out my car and they came over. "Now, how can we help you tonight?" the man asked, while the woman grinned.

"Do you have any beds available tonight? I won't need any breakfast; I'll be on my way early."

They both smiled in a welcoming manner. "Nonsense! We'll get you fed up no matter the time," the woman persisted.

"I'm really OK for food, thanks, just a room needed for me."

"We sure do have a room! Can we help you with any bags?" I shook my head. Easiest to leave everything in the car for a quicker getaway in the morning.

They discussed prices with me then led me to the back of the house. There was a little one-room building with a bed, desk and lamp, no toilet. They stated that there was a type of outhouse next to the shed.

My plan was to leave early in the morning. I hadn't eaten since I died at the bank; I planned on getting food when I made it to England, and if I died of starvation before then, no biggie. I set an alarm, and as soon as my head hit the pillow, I was out – what an exhausting day.

I woke up at 6am to the beeping of my alarm. It was pitch black in the room. I put my clothes on and opened the door. At my feet sat two plastic boxes with a note that read:

'Here are some on-the-go bites you can take with you on your drive. I hope you enjoyed your stay'.

The boxes had pastries and fresh bread balls. Now I felt awful for being a celiac; usually, I'd just take them to see what it tasted like after all this time, but I didn't really have the time to die today. I picked up the boxes to take back to the Shawnies; there was a young lad cutting the grass, maybe around fifteen years old, he looked up and saw me, instantly averting his gaze – I guessed he wasn't allowed to speak to guests.

I knocked the front door of the house, but there was no answer. I stood on the porch and looked around. I noticed a rusty, dark blue pick-up truck with a 'for sale' sign in the side window, asking for £1,300. I heard some clanking coming from one of the sheds; maybe someone was there. I started walking towards it and the man, Mr Shawnie, came out wiping his hands with a cloth.

"Ye right!" He smiled at me. I explained that although I was grateful, I couldn't eat the food, to which he replied, saying that his lunch was now sorted for the day. I also enquired about the truck; I could've afforded it but thought it was best to keep the money I had, so instead swapped him my car and £200, which he was ecstatic about.

I moved my bags into the truck but left my phone and bank card in the other car. I needed to be off grid, just for now. Then, I drove off towards England with a boom and creak from my new old car.

ELEVEN

I got around forty-five minutes into England when I stopped at a Mottobreak. Mottobreak had branches all over the UK and were basically big pit stops filled with fast food, travel shops, truck stops and sometimes, if it was big enough, a hotel. I filled the truck with petrol and decided to go stretch my legs and find some food. I had the choice of Burgersss or Chickin' It, both really dirty, greasy fast food – why couldn't there ever be a fast food branch that did healthy, fresh food?

I decided to go to Burgersss as I heard they had a new gluten-free bun. Walking about the court, about to take my last bite, I noticed that the TVs throughout the walkway had an urgent message screen; I looked at it for around two minutes before the screen jumped to the top left corner and the main area was taken up by a reporter sitting at a table. He coughed to clear his throat; his hair wasn't fully in place and he didn't look prepared to be announcing at all.

"We come to you with an urgent broadcast regarding a dangerous person roaming the UK." It flashed to a security camera image; it was a picture of me in the hospital with the cap on, before I got my hands on the sunglasses, then flashed to an old selfie of myself and Shannon, having blurred her face out. "If you see this person, *do not approach*. You must phone the police and protect yourself – she is *not to be dealt with*." I quickly threw my hood up and pulled the tassels tight. It seemed like I was the only person that saw the report, so I was probably fine, but I rushed out of the building, anyway.

Why would they say I was dangerous? I hadn't done anything wrong. Was this what their reaction was to my condition? I wasn't someone to be feared; I was completely harmless, actually.

I put my sunglasses and cap back on and sped away, looking for more back roads to take. Surely, I couldn't disappear in a big city now? There would be at least someone that recognised me. Maybe I should've gone to the highlands. I needed a new plan.

I had been driving through farmland in silence for hours, trying to calm down, trying to come up with a plan, when I finally put the radio on again. The reporter was talking about me, describing me and saying what to do. He never said my name. He spoke of a viral video of me so I had to stop the car to check my phone, searching for it and remembering I didn't have one anymore. "*Fuck*." I rested my head on my hand; the radio played the audio from the video.

"Yeah, errr, she ran out in front of the car and we hit her, completely caving in her skull. My girl went tae git help and I stayed with the body. She didnae have a pulse or ettin' but then the yin got up and all injuries were gone, it wis mad, eh. She just git up 'n' drove away." The reporter said that the dashcam footage showed clearly that it was me and that you could hear the crunching of my skull very clearly. Double fuck. He stated that some people thought it was a conspiracy and that I was an alien, whereas others thought the whole alert had been staged. He urged people to look up the news reports to see my pictures to be aware of who to avoid, when they weren't driving, of course.

I continued driving the outskirts, dirt roads and farming areas, heading closer and closer to the shore. It was 8pm and getting pretty dark when I came across Shallow Halls, a very small village situated right next to the ocean. It consisted of a few small businesses and homes, and it didn't seem very modern. I decided I'd be able to stay here without being detected.

My first stop was a local shop still open until 9pm. I pulled on my sunglasses and hat, trying to keep my head down. I picked up some food and hair dye. The woman at the till tried to look at my face and I felt panic wash over my whole body.

"Not from around here, ahe? What ye doing through here?" I looked up at her; a small, outdated TV hung from the wall behind her, only showing black and white scribble, blaring white noise.

"I'm just passing through, little road trip. TV trouble?" I asked, trying to dig around for information in case I'd get spotted. She looked back at the TV and pointed her hand over her shoulder.

"Nah, we don't get TV or phone lines over here; most people watch DVDs, and I just like the noise; everyone is at the pub this time of night." She looked at me while ringing my products through the till; I didn't want to seem evasive so I looked back – she had what the Americans would call a 'soccer mom' look: she had a thin front fringe, golden blonde dyed hair, with her brown roots pouring out, all tied into a high ponytail.

I was super relieved to hear that they were somewhat secluded and cut off; I should be safe here for a good while. The shop didn't even seem to stock newspapers.

"If you're looking for somewhere to stay, there's a hotel next to the beach called The Beacher. They'll certainly have rooms; you won't miss it if you follow the road straight through."

I nodded, gathering my items in my arms, nearly dropping the lot. "Thank you very much."

"Oh, and you should go to the pub; everyone will be happy to chat to you. It's right across from The Beacher." That didn't sound good to me, but maybe I should test the waters and see how long I could stay here, depending on if anyone seemed alarmed or not. It'd be nice to be able to set up shop for a little while until I came up with a new game plan.

I got to the hotel. A young man, wearing a black tracksuit with white colour blocking and a black cap, was at the counter, leaning with his back arched and his stubbly chin leaning on his hand. When I came through the door, he huffed. "Claire called and said someone might be coming over, room for one?" I nodded. "Please, yeah." He let out a sigh again and grabbed a pair of keys out of a lockbox. He must've only been in his early twenties but should've grown out of the moody stage by now. He threw the keys at me, which fell to the floor due to me not being prepared. He rolled his eyes. "£20 per night, just pay per day. I'll need the first twenty now." He put his hand out and I gave him the note. He dangled his arm and nodded in the general direction of the upper balcony.

The purple tab on the keys said '*Room 15*'. I put the key in and unlocked the door, but the door stuck upon entry. I used the side of my body to budge it open which made it fly, and I fell in, dropping my purchases on the floor. I turned the light on and closed the door. The light, wooden desk was very dusty and the little lamp with the light yellow covering flickered orange when I tried to turn it on; obviously it was broken, so I switched it back off again.

There was a small double bed against the wall to the left; it had light yellow bedding with pink flowers on it. It also had a small bathroom with a shower. The room was bigger than the Shawnies' but it was more outdated and very dirty in comparison; still, at least it had its own bathroom. I got straight to work with the box of dye – goodbye to my black hair, hello to being fiery ginger. Yes, the colour would pop and grab people's attention, but they wouldn't suspect it had been dyed because who would want to be ginger, really?

After an hour or so, the job was done. My hair was bright orange. My whole life, I'd never changed my hair colour, and now here I was, having changed it so drastically, out of necessity, of course.

I stared at myself in the big mirror across from the bed. I couldn't believe how different dying my hair made me look. I sat down, still staring, and thought about everything that had changed and led me to this moment. Why did my life have to go so mental? I was so happy where I was; now I was just numb, scared and confused all the time. Why was this happening to *me?*

TWELVE

It was so dark out that I had to get near the door to be able to read the sign on the bar: 'orner Tavern'. There was a shadow where a 'C' used to be.

I got to the large, green door and took a deep breath before stepping in; this was the moment I'd find out if I'd be safe here or not, for the time being.

The bright lights hurt my eyes upon stepping inside the bar. The receptionist from before was laughing with some locals.

The heavy door slammed behind me, making everyone turn around and stare. The receptionist's jaw dropped, and he pushed his friends aside, following me to the bar like a puppy. "I-I didn't catch your name before," he said, touching my arm before I reached the counter.

"You never asked… do you need it for the reservation?" Everyone was quiet and still staring.

He shook his head. "As long as people pay, it doesn't matter." I turned to continue walking. "I'm Barry, by the way." He smirked and winked at me – was he trying to chat me up? "I'm sorry for being rude earlier; Claire had woken me up. Owning a hotel makes your pattern weird." He stood tall and proud; I was certain he was trying to impress me. I nodded and continued my journey to order a drink while Barry admitted defeat and sulked away. I could hear his friends laughing at him and a few others sniggering around the room.

The bartender was bald, with a long, grey beard; he was very skinny and lanky. He smiled his rotted teeth at me; he reminded me of what I would've imagined a pirate to look like. I never really drank, but I reckoned I needed one now, so I decided on Shannon's drink of choice: white wine. It tasted like vinegar and inspired a gag reflex, but I still fought through as I knew you shouldn't mix drinks.

The whole time, I felt like I was being watched; I was probably paranoid, but I looked around the room just in case. Multiple groups of people were chatting and laughing, not even looking my way. I finally got to the edge of the room and there was a woman, slightly younger than me, sitting in a booth alone. She had dyed jet black hair, black, winged make-up and a black leather jacket on, proper rocker chick. She was staring at me; we locked eyes for what felt like five minutes but must've only been a few seconds. She raised her glass and smiled at me – the shopkeeper cut in my line of view and sat at the bar with one chair between us.

"I'm sorry about Barry," she chuckled. "The men don't know how to act when a new woman comes around." She looked down at the bar, then back at me. "I'm Claire." She extended her arm.

Shit, I needed to come up with a fake name, but what? My eyes darted around the bar; she looked a bit worried for me. I clasped her hand a bit too quickly. "Emily." She seemed pleased that I had spoken to her. We made general small talk for around twenty minutes, trying hard not to give her any details that were too personal.

"Anyway, if you ever have any questions about the area, you can ask me or anyone really – we're all nice here." She got up to go away.

"Actually," I stopped her, "I was wondering what happened to the 'C' on the sign?" She laughed and pointed over at the group of men who were with Barry.

"Bryde." She gestured to him, and he quickly shuffled over. He was wearing a grey flat cap, a cream, knitted sweater and had a short, ginger beard. "Our new friend Emily wanted to know about the sign."

The bartender overheard and tutted. "Right, I'm going in the back until this is over." He put a glass down and sighed, leaving the room.

Bryde rolled his eyes at him. "Captain Bryde." He extended his arm and I accepted. "Long story short, he lost a bet with me." He nodded towards where the bartender had wandered off to. "So, now it's used as an anchor." The whole room giggled; it seemed there was no privacy here, but everyone seemed close and friendly enough. "There, I done the short version, ya sare loser," he shouted in at the bartender. "I'll tell you the rest another time," he said, winking at me.

I must've had around six glasses before I left to go home; I didn't realise alcohol could go down so easily, even when you didn't enjoy it. I felt fine, though, luckily. When I stepped outside, it was pouring with rain. I steadied myself in the door frame, deciding whether or not I should do a runner to my room; I hadn't ran in a while due to being 'on the run', so maybe that could count as some exercise. I mentally prepared myself to run. "Right, OK." I bit the bullet and started jogging towards the hill that led to The Beacher, when I heard someone calling my name.

"Eden." It surprised me, and I slid in the wet and hit the ground. Slowly and steadily, I struggled to get myself back up, and the voice got gradually louder. "Eden, Eden, *Eden*." It was coming from the beach. I turned around and headed towards the voice, now drenched in rainwater. I got to the edge of the concrete before the sand and the voice was still shouting.

"Stop saying my fucking name!" I shouted back. "Come out where I can see you." I received no response. Did this mean I should be running? Did someone recognise me from police reports?

"Eden." The voice was gentler now, and I recognised who it was; it was Shannon's voice. I instantly ran onto the beach, towards the waves, looking around for the voice, tripping over my feet and landing face first in the sand. It was so squelchy; it felt gross and instantly stuck all over my body, the granules crunching in my teeth. It sounded like it was coming from the waves; I needed to go in and find her. I ran straight in without thinking and started swimming towards the voice. Before I knew it, the voice was gone and so was the beach; my ears started ringing and I lost all feeling of my limbs. My mind started flashing back; the rain was exactly like it was that day. My mind brought me back to fighting with the door; I tried desperately to snap out of it, but it wasn't happening – I was trapped in the memory this time. I knew it wasn't real; it was just my mind; it was dark and I was in England – I wasn't back in my car in Scotland; I just wasn't. I had to live out the full memory again before waking up on the edge of the beach with a gasp and a lunge. Did I die again? It was still dark; it must have not been long. I got up and couldn't walk in a straight line, stumbling back to my room, questioning if anything that had just happened was real or not.

THIRTEEN

I was awoken by a demanding need to vomit. Maybe six glasses of wine was too many. I had got back and instantly collapsed in bed. Maybe my experience last night was a drunken experience. One thing was for sure: I wouldn't be drinking wine ever again.

I felt more well-rested than I had the last while. It was dark outside; I wondered what time it was. There were no clocks in the room and, obviously, I didn't have a phone anymore. Even though I felt well-rested, it must've only been a few hours; although, it wasn't raining anymore. I looked at the bed and saw the sandy mess that had been left behind; the events in some form must've happened – some of it would have been real.

There was a knock at the door. Had I been found? Maybe I could survive the drop from the bathroom window without gaining an injury.

"Emily?" Who the fuck is Emily? I quietly stepped to the door and looked out the peeper; it was Barry, standing with his hands in his pockets and shoulders raised to his ears, looking rather shy. Oh, I was Emily, duh! I opened the door, hiding my body behind it and poking my head round.

He straightened his posture. "Oh hey, everyone was wondering if you'd join us again tonight?" I was still wearing my sandy clothes from earlier and my brain was fried, plus I was twitching at the thought of the events that had caused me to be sandy.

"What time is it, like?" I said, yawning.

He glanced at his watch. "7:30pm, miss." Did I really sleep a whole day away? I needed to be more careful and less vulnerable if I didn't want to be caught.

"Sure, I just need to change and eat; I'll maybe be there around nine." I didn't want to be alone after the night I had had before.

I ate a salad that I had bought the day before and showered using the complementary soaps; I'd need to go to the shop and buy real stuff if I was staying here for a while.

I rocked into the tavern for around 9:10pm and ordered a whisky, much better. I sat in the same seat at the bar and most people seemed to be sat in the same places as the night before. Barry came over to join me. "You know this place does food, too? In case you run out of food in your room." He gestured for two more drinks from the bartender.

"I didn't, thank you." The two drinks were sat in front of him; he slid one over to me and grabbed his before getting up to leave. "Hey, I was wondering if I could get new sheets? I got them a bit dirty earlier."

"Sure, no issue; I'll bring them tomorrow." He winked. I was sure young women would find him smooth or charming, but to me, he was young and cocky, but Claire was right in saying that he acts that way because they're not used to new people. My car was the only one parked at the motel and the village must've been dead for me to have slept all day without disturbance.

I sat at the bar drinking glass after glass again, trying to fill my head with nothingness, trying to forget. Now and then, the locals would include me in their conversations, but I was too numb to form anything meaningful to say.

The door slammed and I never strayed my view away from the bottom of my glass. Out the corner of my eye, I saw someone sit down; it was the rocker chick again. She got up and ordered a drink, standing very close to me. She had some sort of rose perfume on and it smelled amazing. Throughout the night, she kept coming closer to me to order and then returning to her seat. Every time I glanced over, she was staring at me; it was intense. I had lost count of how many I had drunk; everything around my glass was getting hazy. I decided that was enough for me, that I'd finish that one and go.

The woman got up again and I assumed she was going to order another pint, but this time was different. She stood next to me and looked directly at me. "You look like you've had a rough day." I looked down at my hands, twisting my ring around my finger. "Don't worry; we're all running from something here." She put her hand on my forearm, just below the elbow joint, and it reminded me of Shannon. It was as if a shock ran all the way through my arm and made my heart jump out of my body. I slowly raised my head and looked at her face; it had turned into Shannon's and, without hesitation, I put both hands on her face and pulled her in and kissed her like I did the first time we kissed in our teens. She grabbed my waist, leaning closer into me. When we stopped for air, she looked at me with a grin on her face, her eyes looking surprised. She took my hand and led me out of the bar.

She led me to her cottage not far from the bar. I looked at the stars in the sky and could hear a voice in the waves again. "Eden, don't." It was calm and soft and I could barely make the words out. "Come stop me then," I mumbled to myself. The woman didn't seem to notice. We got inside of her home; she never turned any lighting on and I couldn't make out any features of the home. She took off my shirt and pushed me back onto the bed, taking off my trousers and underwear. She put her hand on my chest to keep me down as she got undressed, then mounted my body, kissing everywhere and making out with me. She grabbed my arms and pinned them down while she went down on me. Her face was always Shannon's but flicking from her dark black hair to Shannon's gorgeous blonde locks. Maybe this was Shannon's way of telling me to move on, maybe it was the alcohol; I knew it wasn't her, but I was still desperate for any moment of Shan's face, even if it wasn't real. When I finished (which was rather quickly, having been looking at Shannon), I let out an: "Oooh, Shannon," but the woman took no notice. I fell asleep pretty much straight off.

I woke up with the morning light shining in my face. The woman was standing at her mirror fixing in some earrings. "Morning, sexy." She looked back and winked at me. I sat up and put my hands on my head to try and stop it from pounding. "For future reference, my name is Nadine, not Shannon."

I felt myself go red with embarrassment. "Sorry about that." She shrugged her shoulders and skipped over to her wardrobe to fetch some clothes. I must've looked a mess; I could feel my hair poking out everywhere. I stood up and the room started spinning, instantly knocking me back down; thankfully, she didn't notice. I needed to go but I sat to get myself together before trying again. "Last night," I cleared my throat as I was very groggy, "last night, you said: 'we're all running from something'. What did you mean by that?"

She chuckled. "If I told you, I'd have to kill you."

I rolled my eyes and thought to myself, *yeah right, you could try*. She saw me roll my eyes but must've assumed it was because of how cheesy it was. "And you are running away from a husband because you realised you were gay *or* you're running away from a shitty marriage with your wife, am I right?"

I stared at her – who was she to assume my life? "Not everything appears as it seems." Boy, did I know that. "My wife passed away."

She turned to stare at me. "Damn, I thought you were more scandalous than that." She didn't even apologise for assuming, at least she stood by her decision, I guess. "Anyway," she put her hands on my thighs and brought her face close to mine for what I thought was going to be a kiss, but instead she whispered, "you need to go; some of us have jobs." She slapped my legs and I jumped up, getting ready quickly as she continued fixing her attire in the mirror, trying to show more cleave'. As I walked behind her to leave, she stated, "Don't be a stranger at the bar." She blew me a kiss and I left.

FOURTEEN

I felt dirty; I felt as if I had cheated. My heart belongs to Shannon; I didn't want to give my body or any other part of me to anyone else. I really did see her, though. I knew it couldn't be real, but I so wanted it to be. It was all so vivid and real; she even stopped smelling of roses and instead smelled like Shan.

I returned to my room and noticed the bedding had been changed; I instantly felt super uncomfortable and dashed to the front desk. Barry came from the back, head buried deep in a magazine; he looked up, and with his face sparking up, he threw the magazine on the counter.

"Emily! How can I help you?" he said, leaning into the counter.

"I just wanted to say, if you're going to deliver any bedding or towels, to hand them to me or leave them outside the door? Sorry, nothing against you; I just like my space being for *me*, you know?"

He nodded. "No problem, noted for next time." I turned to leave when he conversed further. "So, that means you'll be staying a while, eh?" I shrugged.

I got back to my room to wash and change. I decided to grab a warm lunch at the Corner and hoped that Nadine wouldn't be there.

When I arrived, Claire was sitting on her own and waved at me. "Hey, Emily, come join!" I sat down. "I'm on my break, just ordered food if you'd like to join for lunch?"

"Sure."

Shortly after, the bartender brought round a rather large steak for her. I stared at it and thought how unfair it was that the cow had to die while I got to live and for forever, it seems. Did this mean I was going vegetarian? I was suddenly disgusted by the thought of eating something dead, maybe because I now knew what it was like to die.

Claire was waving in my face, and I shook my head out of my deep thought. "Huh? Sorry."

The bartender huffed and asked, "Would you like any food, girl?!" I decided on just a baked potato today. Certainly, my mindset had changed, which wasn't the best if I needed to be on the run, but I'd manage.

I didn't stay for drinks in the bar that night, although I did buy a bottle of whiskey from Claire's shop. I needed to come up with a long-term plan. I'd probably need to leave now, although I wanted to find out why I saw Shannon in Nadine, but having made that kind of connection with someone – when I was supposed to be keeping to myself – was very dangerous. I decided that I would pack up and leave within the next two days.

FIFTEEN

I was awoken by a knock on the door. I looked out the eye hole; it was Nadine, wearing her trademark leather jacket.

"Shit." I let out with a sigh before opening the door.

"Hey, work is closed today; we're going out," she said, dangling her car keys.

I hesitantly agreed and let her wait in the car while I got ready. "I don't want to stray far, though, OK, Nadine?" I said, while entering.

"You can trust me," she said, crossing her eyes and sticking her tongue out. She was very pretty, and if I were interested in seeing other people, I'd even have said she was sexy. She seemed too lively to be living there, but as she said, I guess we all had our reasons. "Didn't see you at the bar last night?" she queried.

"Yeah, I just needed a night in really. Any hints as to where we're going?"

She took one hand off the wheel and tapped her nose with her index finger. "Somewhere fun." I really wasn't sure about this; I didn't know who I could trust right then. My curiosity about her took over when I agreed to join her. "And don't worry; no one will see us." She seemed to have grasped that I was hiding from something; I just hoped she didn't know and wasn't taking me to the police; although, the easier option would have been to phone them and have them raid the hotel, so I just hoped the worst wasn't to come. We didn't pass any cars; the clock on the dashboard said it was 11am, so I really was in the right area to be hiding, for now at least. We passed a roadside-type diner about thirty minutes into the journey, and around fifteen after that, we arrived at our destination. I noticed that the whole trip she had stayed Nadine and not changed to Shannon, maybe that was a one-time thing?

The building had signs and posters that said things like 'rest stop' and 'arcade!' But nowhere stated a business name. Surely, an arcade wouldn't get much business this far out? Even so, it's too public to risk.

"Can we go back please? I can't—"

She huffed at me and pointed at a sign. "It's closed today."

I squinted at the sign as she got out and walked to my side, opening the door. "Trust me yet?" She extended her hand to help me out, which I hesitantly accepted. She walked me to the door, holding my hand and cuddling my arm with her other arm. She used a key to get in.

She instantly walked behind a desk and switched some switches that were out of my sight and the whole place came to life. "Heads up." I spun around, and she chucked a bottle of whiskey – which I somehow caught – of which I instantly took a swig. For someone who didn't like drinking, I feared that, after three days, I was on my way to becoming an alcoholic.

She climbed onto the counter. "Which game first?" She clapped her hands together. "*Oh!* Let's bowl." She jumped off the desk and led the way, running, while I downed a lot more of the alcohol. I was so uncomfortable; I needed drink to get through this; I needed to let go and stop being so anxious for once in my life. She set up a lane and sat on my lap and took the bottle out my hand, taking a drink herself. It was only then I noticed that I had drunk half the bottle already. "Drink up – there's plenty more." She turned to face me and tried to kiss me, which I returned with a peck. She got up and took the first turn. Landing a spare, she spun round and bowed.

I took my turn and turned around to look at her reaction, but she had gone; I thought she had been quiet for too long. I went to look and see if she was in the room behind the shoe counter, where she jumped out from behind, shouting, "Ahhh!" and making me jump, only she wasn't Nadine anymore. She slammed another bottle on the counter and jumped up to sit next to it, wrapping her legs around me and grabbing my chin with her finger to bring me closer to her face, kissing me so passionately, exactly the way Shannon did. I missed her so much. It was awful of me, but it was as if I was making new memories with her, and I just wanted life to be like this, for this moment to last forever.

Life owed me a little break at the very least. Maybe I could live out this second life with Shan in Shallow Halls and only deal with Nadine sometimes. Was it so bad to ask for happiness back in my life after so long and the destruction I'd been through?

I knew it wasn't Shannon; it was her body but Nadine's words and actions. Maybe Shan was trying to take control of her body and, I knew it was selfish, but I hoped that was the truth, not that Nadine or anyone deserved to lose their life, but I really needed her back. She could tell me what to do about everything and we could be happy. When I was with her, I felt like I would be nothing without her around. Obviously now, I saw that I was a little something, even if I contributed nothing apart from being a large, red flag on the police radar, of course, for reasons I still didn't understand yet.

She stared at me while I was in thought. "Is this something I need to get used to?"

I looked at Nadine, still looking like Shan, sitting across from me in the lane seats. "Huh?"

She giggled at me. Shannon's smile was so perfect; I used to do anything to make her happy.

"You travelling off to another planet in thought."

I shrugged at her. "I zone out sometimes, nothing to worry about."

She walked over to me and pushed my hair back, petting it. "You're my girlfriend; I'm allowed to worry about you." At first, I took no notice, as I was in Shannon land. *Girlfriend?!* I didn't agree to that. I wasn't ready for that. But I couldn't say no, her face; it was Shannon's. She leaned down and kissed me: biting my lip at the end.

SIXTEEN

I slept most of the drive home. When I woke up, Nadine was completely herself.

"Won't you get into trouble for driving having drunk?" She took her eyes off the road and looked at me, which made me nervous. Even though death wasn't a direct threat to me, I still didn't want to go through it.

"There are never police around here. The closest police station is ages away and they never come because there's no crime here."

We got back to hers and she instantly started making out with me and taking my clothes off. It wasn't the same as when she was Shannon, but I figured I should give her a chance now if I was really going to go through with being with her. I didn't really understand where Shannon had gone.

Nadine obviously knew what she was doing and, as I said, she was very pretty, but my heart still belonged elsewhere, so none of her tricks landed as she planned for them to. She always insisted on pleasuring me and never let me return the favour, the opposite of me and Shannon; she was always to be pleased and she rarely pleased me, which was OK because she deserved to be treated like a queen.

*

I was lying on the beach in Shallow Halls when I saw Shannon run out of the water with her board. I instantly jumped up and ran towards her. She threw her board onto the land and stayed in the water with her arms out wide. I ran in and grabbed her tight, only looking up after a few minutes to passionately kiss her, with both hands on either side of her face. She put her hands on my shoulders and pushed me down until I was on my back under the water. She put all her weight on my body. I fought, trying to hit her arms to tell her I was drowning. This wasn't play fighting – was she trying to kill me? I could see her laughing through the water, but all I could hear was water as I felt it mix with the sand and fill my ears, water pouring into my lungs, no, not again! Please! I tried screaming, but nothing but air bubbles came out. I wasn't dying; it was just getting more and more painful – it was horrible. I could hear a muffled voice shouting in the distance, and with a flash of black, Shan was gone. I stood up and looked around; there was no one in sight, when I felt a tap on my shoulder. I spun around to look at Nadine, who screamed in my face and started pushing me into the water again. Drowning me for round two, having tag teamed with Shannon. She stuck her head into the water, and I heard her clearly scream, "Emily!"

I woke up to Nadine saying my fake name over and over, rocking my shoulder. I was in a pool of sweat and started heavily breathing. She grabbed hold of me and squeezed tight. "You're OK," she whispered in my ear, before letting me go and looking deeply at my face.

"Aw man, sweaty. I'm so gross; I understand if you don't want to see me."

She grabbed my hand. "Of course, I want to see you! Do you want to tell me what you were dreaming of?"

I shook my head and wiped sweat off my brow. I started to get ready to leave without saying anything. This was crazy: I couldn't use someone like this. Just because she appeared as Shannon sometimes, it wasn't an excuse to toy with her feelings like I had. I needed to end it and stop being such a dick, which also meant I needed to leave.

"Nadine." She perked up. I sat next to her on the bed and held her hand. "I'm sorry but I'm still not ready to date after my wife's death; it was unfair for me to try with you." Technically, it was the truth, even if not the full one. She stared at me in silence with her left eye twitching. I wished she would say something and wondered if this was what it was like for others when I zoned out.

She put her hands through her hair and started laughing violently, escaping one to open the bedside drawer. "You know you asked what I was running from?" She stared through me, still with a wild grin. "I kill the people who hurt me." She pulled a kitchen knife out of the bedside table and lunged quicker than I could move. She drove it right into my stomach; I felt the knife inside my body; the pain sent shivers up my spine and caused me to squeal. I couldn't die but I felt every inch of pain from death – what the fuck? She pushed it in further, causing me to yell louder. She put her nose against mine and kissed my lips while pulling the knife out and this time, lunging it into my throat.

SEVENTEEN

I woke up gasping for air, but instead of lunging, my body twitched. I could feel something heavy on my chest and all I could see were stars. I could hear a metal clanking sound and saw dirt fly and hit my face; it was soft so didn't hurt, but it was still gross. I could hear steps crunching in leaves and I squinted my eyes so that I could see as little as possible, making it look as though my eyes were still closed. There was a silhouette standing atop and I could hear hysteric crying. The silhouette's elbows pointed as they put their hands to their head.

"We could've been great together, you know?" she said through sniffling. "I loved you, then you needed to break my heart and make me kill you, didn't you?" She wailed and dropped to the ground, out of my sight. I stood up; I was in a small ditch which would've served as my grave. I climbed out slowly, trying to be quiet while her back was turned. "Why did you make me do that?!" she screamed. I was trying to watch her so I didn't step in her eyeline. Not watching where I was going, my feet crunched some leaves. She turned around very slowly as I froze in place. She looked at me, then glanced in the ditch, puzzled. "Emily? Oh! Emily! Baby." She raised her arm and started walking towards me, with a caring look on her face. In blinks, she flashed from herself to Shannon and to herself again.

I was getting distracted by Shannon when I needed to run, so that's what I did, sprinting away as Nadine grabbed her shovel and followed me. I wasn't awake enough to run properly yet, and my mind was everywhere. She followed my pace too well. I ran through the trees until I hit a road. The tops of the trees made shelter over the road and added shadows to the dark night. I decided the safest bet was to follow the road. I ran for a further twenty minutes, I estimated. My legs were burning with pain and my throat felt like it had shrivelled up from lack of hydration. I hadn't seen anyone behind me for a while but didn't want to stop. Not long after the twenty minutes, a modern car came towards me on the road. I flailed my arms, stood in the middle of the road and waved them down until they stopped. A young couple, I guessed; the girlfriend was driving. They rolled down the window.

"Please, someone is chasing me; I need help," I said, panting. The passenger nodded and I jumped in the back. "Please go, just anywhere, I need to get away."

They sped the car further up the road. They both glanced at each other and the male cleared his throat. They locked the doors, which I thought was strange. "We know who you are," he said to me while looking through the mirror. "We're going to take you to the police." I instantly lunged forwards and grabbed the wheel, pulling it far to the bottom left, causing the car to swerve off the road and straight into a tree. It launched me forwards and straight through the windscreen towards the tree.

*

I woke up behind the tree further down a short hill. I couldn't see the car nor the passengers; I hoped that I didn't seriously hurt them. Surely, they'd be OK due to them having been wearing seatbelts. I wondered how long it had been. I looked down at my legs and noticed my right leg was mangled, my knee facing to the inside of my legs and my foot completely backwards. My leg that was numb before now had a fire of pain shoot up the entire length. I screamed at my leg and grabbed it, not believing it was real, making it worse. I very quickly felt sick and projectile vomited onto my leg and lay back down.

*

Waking up again in the same spot, I slowly sat up with my eyes closed, hoping it had been a dream, opening them to realise it was not. The vomit had now dried onto my trousers. The crash didn't kill me this time. All I could think was *man, I fucking hate cars.* I needed to leave the area before anyone found me. I dragged my body along the ground towards the closest tree and used it to stand myself up, only to instantly fall from not being able to put weight on my leg. Round two. I steadied myself up against the tree, hanging my leg above the ground. I started hopping away from where I came. It wasn't long until I realised that hopping would get me nowhere. I decided I would have to use my gammy leg – not good. I started putting pressure on my leg, trying to walk on it, screaming all the way. It was the worst feeling. Dying was horrible: experiencing death and feeling everything, every bit of pain. But this was up there with it all, although my life hadn't been the best experience in general recently.

Sweat was dripping from my head; I was panting and needed to stop every so often to steady myself and rest against a tree. I was getting nowhere this way, and I really needed to escape the area. If I were to leave without being found, I would need to fix my leg, and there was only one quick fix: death. I hopped and struggled until I found a road. I stood by and waited against a tree.

Along the stretch of road, I saw a large delivery lorry going at top speed. This was my chance. I made sure I wasn't visible behind the tree, before jumping out last minute, left leg first, hopping to right leg – causing my broken bones to crunch and grind together – and diving straight in the way, to get slapped by the metal grates on the front.

*

I woke up face first on the ground with my mouth filled with leaves. I got myself up into a push-up position and spat out the leaves, then hopped up into a standing position. I shook my leg, then danced on it, giggling while doing so.

"Wha—"

I spun around to see the lorry driver frozen in place with shock. I calmly smiled at him. "How long was I out?"

He slowly blinked at me. "About thirty minutes."

I turned around and headed towards the trees on the opposite side.

"Oi!" I stopped and shrugged at him. "You weren't breathing."

"Well, I am now, thanks for your concern." I walked until I was hidden from sight by the lorry, then started running before he asked any more questions.

EIGHTEEN

I had been walking in the forest for hours. I was tired. My legs were giving up beneath me. I was wheezing due to dehydration, and I was close to passing out. The forest was dark but peaceful; the only life was from the odd squirrel, hedgehog or bird, all of which wanted nothing to do with me.

After a while, I noticed that the crunching of leaves had doubled but remained in time with my steps. I tried to look behind me without it being too obvious. Nothing. I continued onwards, single crunches for five steps before it doubled again. I stopped and quickly turned around this time. Still nothing. Maybe I was hallucinating due to the dehydration. This time, I started walking in the direction I came. Crunch, crunch, crunch, crunch, crunch – a man dressed in all black stepped out from behind a tree. He jumped when he realised where I was.

"Miss Dyson." He raised his hands above his head. I darted in the opposite direction and started sprinting away while he quickly followed. "Miss Dyson, Miss Dyson! I mean you no harm, please." He had a bit of an accent but I couldn't pinpoint where it was from and I wasn't in a position to ask. "Miss Dyson!" No one was on my side at the moment. I couldn't trust anyone or let my curiosity win; I'd already made that mistake. I stumbled while I ran; shin splints kicked in and made me feel like a doll, with the non-flexed limbs, moved into motion.

I tilted my head to the side as I ran and shouted, "It's *Mrs* Dyson, call the right fucking name." My voice was croaky. I was over-salivating. My legs wanted to give up.

"Sorry, Miss, eh, Mrs, please stop!" I ran onto a road and got cut off by a white van, of which the doors slid open, showing more men in black trying to grab me. I skidded and changed direction.

"Ugh, we didn't want to hurt you!" The man stopped at the van and quickly rifled in his inside pocket.

BANG.

NINETEEN

My lunge was stopped by someone grabbing my arms. I opened my eyes to see the man that was chasing me close to my face. I shook my body out of his grasp and a further four arms from behind me grabbed me and pinned me down. I was in the back of a van which was rumbling and bouncing all over the place.

"Miss Dyson, we are friends; I promise."

I squirmed some more. "Doesn't fucking feel like it."

The man raised a finger as if he was going to make a point but was interrupted by the van shaking, causing everyone to fall from their place, which I took as my chance to grab the back door handle and burst out the doors of the moving vehicle. I landed funny on my leg which caused me to fall and hit my head on the concrete. Behind me, I heard the man scream, "Stop the van!"

I got up as quickly as I could, the ground shaking and changing direction, going diagonal instead of straight ahead. I felt so dizzy and lost. I tried to collect myself and started running, even though I couldn't grasp directions while my vision was taking me everywhere. "I don't want to keep doing this!"

BANG. A gun, again.

*

I woke up this time unable to move at all. I was tied up. Two men in all black stared at me. How did they know about my condition? Twice they'd shot me, leading to an instant kill, both times expecting me to awaken. They both rolled their eyes over and shoved the main man, who had his back to everyone. "You're awake!" He put his hand on my shoulder. "It's going to be a while before we reach our destination. You can either wait or we can kill you to pass the time." There was no way I could sit through this, knowing what my anxiety was like; I'd have too much running through my head and I'd stress out, so I chose to die. The man put a gun to my head, turning his view away from me to pull the trigger.

TWENTY

I woke up, jolting forwards and hitting my face on the side of the van. I looked around, dazed. The men appeared to have just woken up as well. One of the men had long, black hair and bright blue eyes. I whispered to him, "Where are we going?" He shook his head. "Why not tell me? I can't go anywhere." He looked away to the main guy, who tumbled towards us in the moving van, steadying himself on the long-haired man's shoulder.

"He's not allowed to talk to you, Miss Dyson." He looked towards the front of the van. "Besides, we're nearly there." I squinted my eyes at him. I hadn't been Miss Dyson for years; I didn't know this man – he had no right to call me that. It's so rude to dismiss my whole life with Shannon as if it didn't exist.

The van took a sharp turn, throwing everyone to one side, the long-haired man landing on top of me, instantly raising his hands like he had committed a crime. He backed away from me, nearly clutching on to his side of the van. The van then abruptly stopped, making everyone's heads bob. The driver got out and opened the sliding door at the side. I was nudged to get out of the van. In front of me was a mansion like I'd never seen before; it was huge. A beautiful water feature covered in vines sat in front of the main door. Two men grabbed my shoulders as the other two cut the ropes. The driver then moved to my back and grabbed on to my shirt, the three of them making me walk forwards towards the door, with their boss leading the way. They opened the door and threw me onto the marble floor, hitting face first. I heard a voice shouting, "Oi! Don't you dare!" followed by shuffling feet. I looked up. My vision adjusted to the light and I saw a man paying the boss before him. His gang then left through the front door and I heard the van drive away.

It was now me and the man, alone. He crouched down and tilted up my head. "Hey, partner!" He smirked. He looked like my friend Johnny, but I couldn't be sure. I couldn't trust my eyes anymore. I furrowed my brow. He took a step back, looking surprised. "Do you not recognise me, *bean*? It's Johnny."

I pounced on him, hugging him tight. This time, my eyes weren't deceiving me, and for a moment, I felt relieved to see a familiar face. "Man, am I glad to see you!"

He squeezed me back and sighed with relief. "I'm glad you're alright," he said, petting my back. "You're all over the news." I stepped out of the hug, confused about how this had happened in the first place. I knew he was rich but not 'secret agents at his discretion' rich, and why would he go through all that effort to get me here? "You must be so full of questions – why don't I get you settled in your room? You can get changed and we'll get you fed, eh?" He gestured in a vague direction up the stairs. I nodded and he led the way.

He opened the doors and spread his arms wide. "This will be your room." He smiled at me. "We weren't sure about sizes but we got you a tracksuit for now, then tomorrow, a stylist will take your measurements and get you some clothes." He gestured towards a neatly folded pile of clothes on the bed. "Also, feel free to have a shower whenever – towels are in there. I'll leave you be; see you in a bit." It was a large room with an en suite; the bed frame was one of those with a roof. There was a walk-in wardrobe with nothing in.

After showering, I had to decide whether to put my underwear back on or to go commando under the joggies.

I found my way downstairs to the dining room. The table was large and made of dark brown wood. As far as I could count without focusing too much, I think there were twelve seats. There was a golden candelabra which was lit.

Johnny came from the opposite doorway and clapped his hands together. "Great! You're here! Let's dine." He was followed by a chef, carrying multiple plates and bowls. He sat at the head of the table, and I sat on the seat closest to his left. The bowls and plates contained multiple pieces of veg, sauce and steak. "This is good steak; you'll love it," he said, while putting a slice on his plate, then reaching to pick up one for me, resulting in me covering my plate.

"Actually, I'm vegetarian now." I nervously laughed.

He looked so different and not just because we were older now. You could tell the money had something to do with him seeming more stylish and better groomed. His body language was also different; he stood very proud, whereas in school, he used to hunch down to hide away from people. He was once my best friend, so I was happy to see him having succeeded in life, but the circumstances of our reuniting left me feeling unsettled.

He explained that he wanted to help me and that I could stay at his for a while.

When I went to walk back to my room for some rest, an ominous glow from one of the rooms caught my eye. The door was already ajar, so I pushed it further open with my foot. The room was dark and felt small. There was a small table with a laptop on and I sat across from it. It was open on a page with writing in bold:

'EDEN DYSON WANTED'.

TWENTY-ONE

Why was he looking me up? Before I let my mind explode with questions, stress and anxiety, I decided to close the door a bit more and read on.

> 'Eden Dyson is wanted for unnatural occurrences, and it is vital for her to be brought in for tests.

> 'DEAD OR ALIVE, THIS PERSON MUST BE RESTRAINED.

> 'Police have been informed that she is a dangerous person – real details have been withheld'.

It further had my picture and a lot of intimate information about me and even a brief section on my marriage with Shannon. Somehow, I didn't think this was a public access website. I backed out of the page, and it featured a list, stating:

> 'Highly secure secret service sector nine.

'MOST WANTED

'AGENTS MUST NOT, UNDER ANY CIRCUMSTANCES, SHOW THIS TO PEDESTRIANS'.

Was Johnny a secret agent? Surely not. He had his big company; he didn't need any more money. Or maybe it was all just a front? It didn't explain why he'd get others to do his job of capturing me for him or why he wouldn't hand me in straight away. I would need to confront him to be sure; maybe I'd need a weapon in case he attacked. I didn't want to harm anyone, so why did I think I'd be able to face my childhood best friend like that?

I read on. There were a lot of names on this list; maybe there were more like me? Or maybe I could find someone that could help. At least I now knew why the police were after me, even if they didn't. I had done nothing wrong. The government just wanted to experiment on me, probably to try to recreate my condition for themselves, which was *very* dangerous. Even more reason to hide.

I continued scrolling through the names:

'Sonny Jules
'Jordan Winter
'Reuben Connolly
'Gorgeous (Geo) Wills
'Isabella Patel
'Dr Ludo Habnossen'

I stopped and clicked on the doctor's file. It stated:

'Dr Ludo Habnossen is wanted for finding and distributing cures for multiple diseases and conditions without the government's permission, resulting in an intake loss for our officials. The doctor went on the run and is now in hiding.

'WANTED DEAD AND ALL BELONGINGS DESTROYED'.

Before I could further examine their life or even see a picture, I was startled by a noise, causing me to close the tab and sprint out of the room. Running round a corner, I crashed into Johnny. "Oh god, I'm so sorry, Johnny!" I said, gasping.

He waved his hand as if to say it was fine. "I was just bringing you a laptop; I thought you'd have been switched off for a while and want to catch up, just don't log in to anything." He seemed genuine, but I needed to remember this man was now a stranger compared to the person I'd once known.

I took the laptop and he started to walk away before I called him back. "Johnny." He spun around to look at me. "Why am I here?"

He looked worried, then let out a breath of air. "I understand that you must feel like you can't trust anyone." He gulped. "But I promise that you're safe here; I'll explain more tomorrow." He looked deep into my eyes, his gleaming with water. "There is a lock in your room if you need." He looked down at his feet and floated away, more like the Johnny I used to know.

I got to my room and hesitated before locking the door. I sat on the bed and opened the laptop, typing into the search engine my name. Endless news articles, pedestrian interviews, forum threads and personal photos appeared before me. I didn't know what to click on first, or what to think.

I first clicked on an article stating that I was a dangerous criminal, wanted because I killed my husband and kids. I rolled my eyes. "Yeah, OK," I tutted.

The next was a video, interviewing pedestrians and asking their opinions on, 'the woman that can't die'. Understandably, they were mostly scared, even without the media and police's scaremongering; a person that couldn't die was a pretty worrying ordeal.

The next was a forum thread all in support of me, saying that I was 'misunderstood' and was most likely scared, which they were not wrong about. With the general public knowing of my condition, surely that changed what sector nine could do?

TWENTY-TWO

For the first time in a long time, I woke up feeling fresh. I had a comfy place to sleep; I was pretty sure I was safe staying here; and I was more at peace in my mind, knowing that I couldn't be chased due to the public's knowledge.

I got up to answer a knock on my door. A woman burst through, wearing a black dress, thick black glasses and sporting a short blonde bob. "Right – arms out," she demanded through her purple lipstick. She looked at my confused expression, rolled her eyes and sighed. "I'm the stylist." I moved into the various positions she barked at me, while in-between measuring my body and limbs.

She got up and popped her back straight, doing laps, looking me up and down a few times over. She finally stated, "I'll be back with a wardrobe tonight," before strutting out of the room.

Johnny wasn't in during the day, so I spent the day exploring his home, every so often flipping an ornament to check if there were any secret buttons to hidden rooms, but he seemed clean. Passing my 'detective' skills was pretty easy, though, even now when I was supposed to have my guard up.

The stylist returned before Johnny did. She had a full wardrobe's worth of clothes but insisted on me wearing this dark green dress for the night; she was very persistent, so I put it on, if only to make her go away. Before I could close the door after her, Johnny slid into view, instantly raising his hands to his mouth. "Wow, you look so gorgeous," then raised his arm out for me to link with. He was wearing a white tux with a purple bow tie.

"Where are we going? I can't go anywhere, Johnny," I said, feeling a flush flow through me.

"No worries, we're having dinner downstairs," he said with a wide grin. I trusted him and linked arms, letting him lead me downstairs.

Getting down, half the table was covered with a feast of vegetables. We helped ourselves to food. I didn't quite understand what the occasion was, but I thought I'd stay quiet to keep him happy.

"So," Johnny cleared his throat, "I brought you here because I saw that you were in trouble and I wanted to help." He grabbed my hand at the edge of the table. "But I need something in return." Oh no, here it was, he was going to want to gain my condition for himself – I should've known. "Eden, you must know that I've always been in love with you?" A sharp jab struck in my heart and I sat back in shock. "Oh, maybe not – anyway, I understand that you could never feel the same for me because of my gender, but…" Shannon was right all along and I was too blind to see, or maybe I just didn't want to know, "I'd like for you to marry me." He got down on one knee and revealed a gold ring with a rather large diamond on it. "You wouldn't need to be physical with me apart from in public, and I would never force you into anything. You'll live forever, so those years will do nothing to your life, but it would make me so unbelievably happy, and you'd always be protected by me legally. Plus, when I pass, you can take my fortune and it'll get you by." He sighed a breath of air as if a weight lifted from his shoulders. Looking at my shoes, he added, "I know it's a lot, so I'll let you think about it." I tapped his shoulder and left, speechless.

I knew he was just trying to help, but who the fuck did he think he was? Did he think I needed a man to swoop in and save the day? I couldn't fucking die; I was pretty sure I'd could be independent. If he really wanted to help me, there wouldn't be conditions tied to it.

I went to hide in my room; the blanket of safety that I felt this morning was stripped away. No one seemed to be trustworthy; this was so hard. My thoughts were interrupted by a knock on the door. "Hey, I just wanted to let you know that I'll be out for the night – help yourself to anything in the house," he said through the door.

I waited around half an hour before leaving the room. So many thoughts and feelings, my head was bouncing; I couldn't keep up – my anxiety was pushing harder than usual. I found his alcohol cupboard and started drinking. I couldn't stop. After the third bottle of whisky – which I accidentally smashed against the counter – it was gone, time to move on to something new. Vodka. I was already seeing in blurs, but my thoughts had slowed down, so I was halfway there – I needed them to stop. Two bottles of vodka did the job. My thoughts had become a whisper and whims screamed instead. I was starving. All I wanted were potato waffles. I had the munchies. Time to go on a mission to find some food. I looked at the doorway and turned to face it. I took my first step forwards, but instead of seeing the doorway closer, I now had a view of the paisley carpet, which was fast approaching my person. *Boomf.* I hit the floor, making my head spin. I used the counter to up and steady myself. Trying again, my legs failed me and started taking me left instead of forwards, causing me to walk into the door frame, grasping on to it so that I didn't fall again. I swung around to face the wall outside of the room. Pictures hung from doorway to doorway in a straight line through the hall and my swing had brought me face to face with one. I squinted my eyes to make the photo come into focus; it was a group of people outside of Johnny's childhood home, but they were all… Shannon? I pushed myself away from the wall, causing me to fall on my arse. Quickly getting up and sprinting in the other direction, I skidded and hit my side on a table, knocking over a vase, and flowers spilled everywhere. I kneeled to pick them up when I noticed Shannon standing at the end of the hallway. I got up and slowly started walking towards her as she did to me. We came face to face.

"I told you and you didn't listen; that's what killed me." It was actually her this time and not Nadine with her tricks.

I started to sob like a child, shaking my head. "No… why would you say that?! No," I cried between gulps and whimpers.

She rolled her eyes, turned away and, with a blink, she was gone, leaving me by myself. "Shannon! Come back!" I called out. "No!" I hit both hands against the wall at either side. "*No.*" Bang. "No!" Smash. My reflection disappeared and was replaced by shattered reflections. I had been looking into a mirror. I put my hand through my hair, stressed out; the drink was supposed to make me feel better, not worse. I took my hand down and noticed it was bleeding. I stared at it as waves of ocean water started to fill my ears; I covered them and fell to the floor. "Nope!" and the water was replaced by all my thoughts, questions and emotions. Time for more drink. I ran and skidded back to the cupboard and grabbed the first bottle within reach, without even reading what was in it. About halfway through downing it, everything disappeared and went numb again. *Let's go out and run* was the next bright thought in my wasted mind. I burst out of the glass doors, letting them fly open, and was met by water right at my feet. "Nooooo!" I screamed. I vomited straight into the water; it tasted disgusting, so I continued to down the bottle in my hand to wash my mouth out. The water formed a giant wave and took me whole.

TWENTY-THREE

I woke up swallowing a gulp of water; obviously, I had died again. Not wanting to know what my predicament was, I opened my eyes slowly. Everything was still blurry and bright blue; I was sure I was facing down. I flipped myself over and was now facing the bright pink sky and enjoying fresh air. I looked around, climbed up onto a ledge and rolled onto my back. Still emotionally drained from the night before, I fell asleep instantly.

*

This time, I awoke to a grey sky raining onto me. I hopped up and looked around, spotting an outdoor swimming pool next to me and the glass doors back into the mansion at the other side of me. I facepalmed. The water I witnessed through the night was just the pool. I giggled it off until panic struck through my entire body – what about the mess I made? I hoped it was all a dream.

I walked through the house, past my path of wreckage, to

find Johnny sitting in an armchair with his head in his hand. He saw me and shot up. "Quite the party you had last night." He gestured to the hallway while walking towards me.

I felt my face go red with embarrassment. "I'm sorry I—"

He cut me off by putting his index finger in the air. "Nothing to worry about here; I've had parties that have ended worse." He laughed and looked at his feet, his face turning serious. "Now," he rubbed my shoulders, "do you have an answer for me?"

"Johnny," I shook my head, "would you really be happy knowing that I don't feel the same?" He nodded his head with a big grin on his face. "Shannon," I sighed, "Shannon was my soulmate, the only person for me, I'm sorry."

His face dropped and his eyebrows furrowed. "Don't give me that shit," he said, slapping his thigh. "Eden, she treated you like crap," he said hysterically. I couldn't believe he had said that, but he was just hurt; he didn't mean it. I looked away from him, avoiding eye contact, and he continued, "She used you. All she wanted was constant attention and servitude and that's exactly what you gave her."

Now this was too far. "*No!*" I said, raising my hand to tell him to stop.

"*Yes*, Eden! You did anything she asked, followed her around, cut off your friends, moved country, stopped talking to me, hey, I bet she never even pleasured you; what *did* she do for you, Bean?" He was agitated.

"Just her existing was enough for me; what our relationship was like is nothing to do with you." Voices were starting to get raised.

"Shut the fuck up with that trash! Even after death she still has a hold on you." He sighed and looked straight at me, locking my gaze. "I'm sorry." He opened up his phone. "I didn't want to tell you this, but she was cheating on you." He showed me his phone, which had two selfies side by side of Shannon and Cassidy, lying naked under a blanket. The one on the left showed Shannon kissing her cheek and the one to the right had them kissing each other. I fell to the floor. How, how could she do this? I thought she *loved* me. As if her death didn't break my heart enough, now this.

TWENTY-FOUR

My mind went silent. All thoughts left and any possible re-entry was blocked.

With a blink, I was back underwater, struggling to breathe, flustering to free myself and failing, blacking out and waking deeper than before. I was reliving the nightmare, only it was worse. It was as if I had a weight, an anchor, holding me down. My chest was tight. Suddenly, my body started swaying as if there were waves pushing me under the water. This time, when I blacked out, I opened my eyes to Johnny shaking me. "Eden?" He sighed a breath of relief.

I pushed myself back, away from him, and scurried towards my room, my chest still tight and suffering from sharp pains. I started packing the clothes into a bag; fuck him – I would take the clothes. I kept stopping intermittently to vomit or catch my breath. Johnny stood in the doorway. "You're seriously going to deny yourself the experience of real love? You could be very happy here." He muttered other threats and negativity like, "What are you going to do on your own?" and "Where will you go?" or "No one else will ever love you the way I do." I really hoped that last one was true; this love I did not want. I don't think I trusted love in general anymore, anyway. I couldn't let myself think about it all yet; I needed to get away.

Johnny left, knowing that his words weren't hitting, and I made my way to the garage. Rifling through a dish for keys, I found one with a bow tie on; the label said 'Mrs Janey', ew. If the car was meant for me then it wouldn't be as bad if I stole it. After all, I didn't want to give the police a real reason to chase me. I threw my things in the back and zoomed away. I had a quick look in the glovebox and found it stuffed with money, lucky for me (for once). I didn't even know where I was, just any direction away was good for now. So, I kept driving until I hit a city. It looked big and busy; it would've been perfect for my original plan to get lost in the people, but there was no way for that to happen now. A loud bloop sound vibrated inside of the car, followed by Johnny's voice. "You know this car is chipped, right? I've told the media where you are and I'm sure the police will follow shortly after." He let out a smug grunt. "Should've taken my generous offer, you bitch."

I gathered the money, burst out the car, grabbed my bag and started running through the city, ditching the car. It was no use, though; I was met by a crowd of reporters and cameras. I could hear multiple voices saying my name and saying a brief bit, before they surrounded me and started throwing questions and shoving microphones in my face. I couldn't see anything through the multiple items blocking my view. I took a deep breath. "OK, OK," I said, raising my hands to ask everyone to calm down. "I need help; I need Dr Habnossen, Dr Ludo Habnossen." Soft mutters arouse from the crowd. "Thank you," I said and pushed my way by them. They started to flow after me, erupting into a roar of questions, which I ignored and ran away from. They weren't very fast because of their gear, so it wasn't difficult to lose them.

I ran towards a train station, jumping the turnstile and sliding onto the closest train before the doors closed. I was still wearing the dirty dress and must've had a funky musk; that, plus the fact I was wanted, made sure that all eyes were on me. The screens weren't working so I had no idea where I was going.

I walked the length of the train and sank into the very end seat with no window, facing the wall. There wasn't even a conductor on this train, so I didn't need to pay for a ticket. I counted the money which had been stuffed in my bag in the rush, thus crumpling it. Around £1,500, that'd get me by for now. Maybe I could buy a car and find a ferry that would take me away.

I waited until the very last stop, hours later, when it had turned dark. It stopped at a place called Besh. Nothing but fields and a small B & B, the perfect place to hide.

I walked in the door of the B & B and it opened up straight into a pub, which had two old men sitting on opposite sides of the room, one with his nose in a book and the other falling asleep. A woman walked in from a back room; she had dyed her hair grey, but she didn't appear quite old enough to be 'going grey'. "Can I help?" she asked, looking cautious.

"Yeah, a room for the night and a whisky, please," I said, taking some money out of my pocket.

She raised her eyebrows while complying and taking what money she needed. "We don't get many folk out here." She shook her head. "And certainly not dressed like that." She looked me up and down and scrunched up her nose.

"I'm sorry, I'd like to just keep to myself tonight." I grabbed my drink and walked to a table alone.

She disappeared and shortly returned with keys, saying nothing and heavily placing them on the table.

I finished my drink and moved upstairs, binning that fucking dress.

TWENTY-FIVE

Today I needed to find a car. In the midst of my frantic packing, I accidentally grabbed the laptop, so I decided I'd use it once and dump it here. I first looked for the closest town or city: 50km away. I then looked on selling sites to find cars for sale in that area – there was only one: a 2008 model selling for £750. I didn't look too much into the details; I just needed a car. Using the hotel phone, I called the owner, who wouldn't be free until the next day. It would take me long enough to hike in that direction, anyway. Before leaving, I thought, *fuck it* and checked my email. Hundreds of emails flooded in. Lots of reporters, journalists and government official emails. One name I didn't expect to see on my scroll was Cassidy Ali. Multiple emails filled with her saying she needed to speak to me covered my screen. One included her number, so I called. She was speechless when I stated who I was, which was good because she just needed to listen. I said I'd drive to her, and she could say her piece.

"Act-actually, I'm in Brigwiggs." She managed to push the words out. I quickly typed how long it'd be to drive from the town back home and told her I'd be two days. I hid the laptop under the mattress and hopped out of the B & B towards the town. A fifteen-hour hike with no water or food would easily turn to twenty hours plus if I were to die. Although, with my time limit, I was counting on myself to hang on and not die this time (when had that ever worked out for me?). Luckily, the walk was a straight line and I didn't have to stray in another direction at any point.

My jeans, trainers and backpack filled with money and clothes made me stick out compared to others I saw briefly in passing, with their large rucksacks and boots. I walked along the roadside as it edged a mountain, only sporadically going up and down in hills. I hadn't seen any cars at all, a good chance for me to lay low.

I walked for hours upon hours. It turned dark. My stomach was growling so much that I imagined it jumping down and having a conversation with me, only I wouldn't be able to join in as my throat had been dried out to a crisp. I thought back at how it may have been a good idea to bulk up on food before I left, but I didn't want to be anywhere for long just now; plus, it meant that I didn't need to stop for bodily functions.

Upon reaching the top of one of the hills, I needed to stop to catch my breath, resting my eyes while hunched over. When I opened my eyes, I saw a car light roll up behind me. It stopped and rolled down the window. "Hey, are you lost? Pretty dangerous to be walking round in the dark." I could only see a blob in the driver's side as my eyes were adjusting to the light inside the car. "Where ya headed?"

"Just the town." I pointed up the road, making him lean closer to the window and open the door.

"That's ages away! Get in." Obviously, I had absolutely no

luck with vehicles and this was a dangerous situation, but all my bones had released the moment he opened the door. I couldn't do that journey much longer. So, I got in.

Driving along, I rested my head against the window and gradually felt my eyes close. As much as I wanted to stay awake, I held no ability to fight it. Soon, I was fast asleep.

I woke up to the feeling of jerking on my trousers and the noise of the man's deep breathing. I opened my eyes to see him next to me trying to take my trousers off. He saw my eyes flash open and instantly climbed over to sit on top of my body, putting one arm across my neck and leaning into it, pinning his body weight on top of me, continuing to try and take down my trousers with the other hand and succeeding. I was crying; I could hardly breathe. Of course, no one could give me one little break; it was too ridiculous to hope for a day without danger.

"Oh yeah, you're a dirty girl, aren't you." He started taking his trousers off and I started throwing my arms wherever I could. His thin, balding hair stuck up. I grabbed the door handle and opened it, causing him to fall out and hit his head. Out cold.

TWENTY-SIX

I opened his glovebox and searched the car, emptying all of his belongings next to him. I even crouched and checked his pulse, still alive. With any luck, the creep would spend the rest of his life in jail.

I drove away. At least I'd be in the town sooner now. There was no radio available out there, so I was left with the sound of the man's voice, the words and grunts, 'dirty girl', swirling through my mind and haunting me. He didn't deserve to live, but that wasn't my call. I wasn't going to intentionally hurt anyone.

Reaching the town, I dumped the car at the entry sign and walked the rest of the way. I found a hotel to lay rest in for the night before travelling off to meet the seller the next day. He had driven it to a local shop's car park where we were to meet, so I saw clearly that it was working. No hassle and no messing around. He tried to speak to me a bit, but I instantly gave him the money and he handed me the keys, and I set off towards Brigwiggs. Even if I had time to speak to the seller; I was still left near speechless from last night's events. I couldn't believe that on top of everything that had happened, this had joined the list. Every time I closed my eyes, my head was filled with images and sounds from both my drowning and this man attempting to assault me, and it was all topped off by the thought of Shannon and Cassidy making a fool of me. I had given my whole life to Shannon, but – and I hate to say it – Johnny was right; what did she really give me? Nothing. I decided to be thankful for the blind happiness I had experienced, even if it wasn't due to truth. Maybe in my never-ending life, I would find someone that would treat me right, but how fair could that be for anyone? Outliving every partner I'd have would be a painful ordeal for everyone involved.

I was driving from pretty much the other side of the UK, so it was set to be a long one, but I'd be there by tomorrow. For sure. The problem of a lengthy journey at this point wasn't only that I may be discovered but also that I was left alone with my thoughts and memories. I wondered what Cassidy would even have to say to me: 'sorry I fucked your wife and made you look stupid'? But I had to know; I needed answers.

All I wanted was a drink. Not the best thing to crave after what had happened last time. But I just wanted my mind to switch off. Evidently, I found it difficult enough to drive without alcohol pulling me down. I thought I should be giving the drinking a miss from now on, seeing as I was a lightweight who hallucinates.

I was deep into England and needed to drive to get back home in Scotland. It was a huge risk going back home, where it all started, where the most people would recognise me, but I was so sick of not understanding my life, so I had to let Cassidy try to give me an explanation for Shannon's actions.

I tried to take as many back roads as possible; I was

travelling in a vague direction which I hoped was towards Scotland. I decided there would be no stops, that I'd drive all day to meet Cassidy. We had arranged to meet at the hills by the hospital; it was a quiet area that would provide good cover. We didn't set a time so most likely one of us would be sitting around waiting for a while; I hoped it was her so that I wasn't staying in the one spot for too long.

Somehow, on this journey I didn't get any hassle: no crashes, no police, no stops, no breakdowns and no one seemed to look at my face.

It was 8am when I arrived at the parking spot between the hills; I was the only person there. Grabbing my jacket, I lay down in the back and had a nap.

TWENTY-SEVEN

I was woken up by the sound of clanking glass. I looked up and there was Cassidy, standing nervously at the window. I glanced at the time; it was now 9:30am. She moved back from the door, and I opened it.

"Well, what do you have to say?" I grunted at her while stepping out.

She looked over my shoulder, unable to look me in the eyes. "I'm sorry," she started. While she spoke, I felt my body become overwhelmed. I wanted to pay attention, but instead I was lost underwater, dying then waking up underneath the man, blinking then being shouted at by Johnny, smashing mirrors, then being surrounded by media, loud murmurs, then thrown into Nadine's knife, all in circles. I zoned in and out to hear odd bits. "We loved each other," and, "I told her, I really did," and finally, "she was going to leave you." My flashes were interrupted by police sirens and, as I came to, I saw blue lights flashing against her face. "I'm so, so sorry, Eden." I looked behind me; two police cars had just pulled up. I quickly backed into the car and started the engine, zooming over the grass and past the cars.

I turned round the bends between the hills and found that two massive blacked-out cars were following me full speed. The one in front had someone lean out the passenger's side and start shooting at me. Were they crazy?! That could cause a serious accident and harm someone. I would stop to protect others, but I really didn't want to find out why the government were so desperate to meet me; I felt everyone would be worse off in that instance.

I put my foot to the floor, zooming by the river bend. I wasn't even watching the road at this point; I was too concerned about these nutters. Before I knew it, I was at the beginnings of the cliff, fuck. It was a case of facing my trauma or being exposed to a new one, so I chose the more familiar option, diving out of my car and sprinting up the hill. Having taken up running over the last few years really did help, but recently, I'd not been able to exercise properly, and I could tell the difference.

I saw a blur of suits dive out of the black cars and even heard bullets driving into the mud around me, before one yelled, "Hold fire!"

I got to the top of the cliff and ran to the edge, peeking over and instantly feeling dizzy. My feet became heavy and felt as if they were sinking into the ground. I looked over the edge and vomited. Shaking, I turned to face a group of people all wearing black suits, pointing guns at me. "Eden Dyson, put your hands up and come with us," one said in a loud, commanding voice. There was no way I could let them take me, so instead, I let my weight go and, with my back to the edge, I floated off the cliff. One of the suits fired a bullet, hitting me in the side. I heard clouds of murmurs and the loud one shouting, "Go, go, go!" This time, I didn't hit the water, and instead, a sharp rock sliced right through my throat.

TWENTY-EIGHT

I woke up, thrusting forwards and smacking my forehead against a shelf. "Agh," I said, grasping my head. The room seemed to rock, shake and sway; I swear, I didn't hit my head *that* hard. I looked around; I was on a small, single bed, parked in-between a wall and a small side drawer, which was against the bed and the wall where the door was, leaving very little room to move or breathe. The room took a big tumble, throwing my back against the wall. Through the wall, I could hear outside *whoosh*, the sound of waves crashing against the walls, causing the place to rock. How did I get on a boat? I wasn't tied up and I was sure the government wouldn't have given me a bed. Someone knocked on the door. I quickly looked around for anything to protect myself with.

Before I could find anything, a woman walked through the door, stopping in her tracks and blinking when noticing me. "Oh hey, you're up." She was wearing dark green cargo trousers that stopped above the ankles and a ribbed beige tank top, her bleached blonde hair flowing over her shoulders. My eyes continued to dart around the room, which she instantly caught on to. "Dr Ludo Habnossen," she said, extending her hand, which I accepted and shook.

"Er, Eden Dyson."

She flashed her perfectly white teeth at me. "I know who you are, but I'm thankful for a formal introduction – I've not met a lot of new people in recent years," she said while tying her hair up into a big, looped lazy bun. "Ready to walk about?" she asked, opening the door. I walked through as she held it open for me, then took the lead walking through the kitchen and up some steep stairs to the main deck, where a man in full camo gear was at the wheel. His ginger hair shone in the sun. "Eden, this is my friend, Kes Wington."

He took his hands off the wheel and faced me. "Ma'am." He shortly saluted before returning to his duty. Man of few words.

The doctor tapped me on the shoulder and guided me back to the kitchen, gesturing for me to sit at the table. She put her hands deep into her pockets and rocked her feet, before sitting across from me. "So, my question to you is: how did you know about me?" She rested her head on her arm.

"How can I know you are who you say you are?" I asked. I felt safe, but I still knew that I needed to be wary of where I put my trust.

"You're the one that asked for me, honey." She stood up and dug around in her bra, pulling out a plastic licence card and handing it to me. It checked out; I don't think she would've forged it. As I said, I didn't feel like I was in a position of danger.

I nodded and handed it back. "I'm sorry, you just don't look like a doctor to me." She instantly rolled her eyes but let me continue talking. "My fr... someone I used to know had hacked into some wanted list and you were on it, not far from me, actually."

"OK, that seems valid, the part about the list, not the 'not looking like a doctor' bit; that, that's bullshit." She made me giggle. I shouldn't really have been judging people on how they look; I was usually wrong when I did, anyway. "So, you can't die, right?" I was reluctant but figured people knew now anyway so nodded. "Interesting." She ducked her head. "You know, we took a huge risk coming out of hiding to find you; you're very lucky we beat the suits to your body." She raised her eyebrows.

"Yeah, that could've been bad news, thanks."

She smirked at my response and stared at my face with her bright blue eyes. "So, before we take you anywhere," she said, tracing her finger around the table; her pause made me unsteady – I felt I needed to prepare to swim, even though I didn't know what was coming, "I need to know why you 'need' me." She used air quotes.

TWENTY-NINE

I had a private conversation with her about what I needed, which she agreed to but informed me that it may take a while to meet my demands and countered with a request of her own for the time it'd take for mine, which I accepted.

"Doctor!" Kes shouted from the top. We both moved up to see him. "We're nearly there, time for the box, ma'am." He nodded towards a large crate behind him.

Ludo turned to me and smiled, putting her hand on my shoulder. "Ready to enter the box?" I glanced at the box and shot back at her, which made her laugh. "Don't worry; I have to go in, too." She went into the open box and gestured for me to come join her, to which I cautiously followed.

"Why?" I asked as Kes closed up the box behind us.

"We're both wanted; we can't risk being seen, and this is the least suspicious way of doing so." She fiddled with the sunglasses hanging from the neck of her tank top, which were making it dip dangerously low, revealing a bit of cleavage, not that I was complaining; she was completely stunning. "Plus, it's best if only Kes knows our secret location so that it's totally secure." The boat swayed and knocked me into her. She caught me by the arms and I could feel myself blushing. I quickly sat down to prevent it from happening again. "When the boat stops, we'll need to be super quiet." She sat opposite me, and I mimicked zipping my lips.

Shortly after, I could hear us docking and Kes speaking another language with a male, before the crate was shoved round and became weightless – I guessed we were off the ground. We then got parked onto the back of something that bounced and squeaked, followed by the sound of chains getting thrown over and wrapped around the crate.

The journey seemed to take a long time, with lots of shaking and bouncing while we sat in complete silence. I decided sleeping was the best choice to pass the time. Every so often, I was awoken by the vehicle hitting obstacles.

When I woke up, the crate was open in a large, silver room where Kes and Ludo were sat at a table eating spaghetti. I got up and sat with them. Kes got up and returned with a plate, which he placed in front of me. "Mrs Dyson." He handed me a fork.

"It's actually Ms Dyson now, but I'd prefer Miss, just call me Eden." Oh, how things had changed now that the truth had come out about Shannon and her sexcapades, hurtful bitch. I looked down at the plate; it looked like tomato and veg, so I started eating. "So, Kes, are you also on the run?"

He looked up at me and sat up straight. "Not anymore, miss." He stood up sharply. "I must return to my position," and he marched away.

"The government thinks he's dead," the doctor continued. "He's very focused on keeping us safe and the military shit has been drilled into him, so forgive him for being blunt." She piled her plate on top of his.

"How did you meet?"

She clanked the plates back down and put her finger to her chin as if to think. "You know, it's a long story. Basically, us both being fucked by the government brought us together, and it's just been the two of us for a good few years now." She took the plates over to a small sink area at the edge of the room. "No contact with the outside world, two-man family in hiding."

I continued to scoff my food. "Why is he hiding?" While I scoffed the rest of my food, Ludo proceeded to tell me Kes's story of how the government took the body of a normal man whom had died of natural causes and transformed it back to life as a completely obedient, single-minded solider/assassin who they used to complete all their dirty work, most of the time not on legal or moral grounds. What they didn't count on was the previous owner of the body's sense of justice and morality breaking through and Private Wington 'dying'. I found it difficult to believe that the government would basically manufacture their own man and call him *Kes*, but Ludo had no reason to lie to me, especially about someone else's story. When I finished my meal, I took it to the sink and did everyone's dishes. Once I had finished up, the doctor clapped her hands together.

"Right, shall we get started?" she asked while gesturing towards one of the rooms. She was very eager, considering we probably had a few years of work ahead of us. She saw my inner questioning. "No time like the present when you want to help people, right?" I nodded; she was right. Might as well pack in as many hours as we could, for the sake of other people. The door had the paint peeling off but, when opened up, inside, it turned into a very clean, nearly metal-looking medical room. "If you could lie down for me, please."

I climbed onto the bed in the middle of the room as Ludo washed her hands, put her coat on and readied a syringe. She instantly turned around and pointed it towards me. "This'll pinch."

"Wow." I put my hand in front of the needle. "What's in this?"

She moved it away from me. "Trust me; you'd feel better if you didn't know." I did trust her; if the wanted report was true, then she was a good woman and my instincts told me to listen to her. I took my hand down and she pierced my skin.

THIRTY

Her side of our agreement was that while we waited for my requirements to be met, we would use my condition to help treat diseases. Not by dispersing my condition to others but rather by injecting myself with one disease at a time, while the doctor worked on cures which she tried and tested on me, and if I didn't die after being injected with a cure, I'd kill myself and she'd contaminate me with the same disease again and the same cure again to be sure that the cure worked.

This first disease was horrible: hot sweats, involuntary muscle spasms and difficulty breathing, only getting worse and worse the longer I had it. After every time it killed me, I felt I couldn't go on with it again, but I never complained; we were doing this for the greater good. Nine months of hard work paid off when we finally got our first cure. That night, the three of us celebrated with alcohol and dancing (Kes didn't dance, of course). When Kes returned to his post, Ludo kissed me. I looked at her in shock.

"What? Do I not look like a lesbian, either?" She rolled her eyes. Why would a woman so beautiful and so good want me? As my life had shown, it was only evil people who show me any form of love. There was no way that Ludo ever had any evil intent, and dying over and over with the same person fighting to save your life kind of gives you a stronger bond than you would have with others. I kissed her back and, in an instant, we were ripping each other's clothes off. Oh, it was the best night of my life. Maybe it was the alcohol, maybe it was the fact that I wasn't sick or maybe I was going stir-crazy, but I believed it was good because finally something in my life was right, when, for the most part, there had been something wrong: my parents, being in the closet, Shannon, my condition, Nadine, Johnny, the man in the car, Cassidy, the government, my condition again (twice because it had really fucked me up).

We spent one full day cuddling in bed before we were back to work with a new virus. From then on out, we were always close; we never spoke about the nature of our relationship, but it never felt needed. She always looked after me, was always caring and made sure I was comfortable, even while she was working her arse off on vaccines, medications and solutions.

We spent six years in hiding, trying to cure diseases, before she finally found what I wanted. After the last disease that we cured, she grabbed my hand. "Eden, I've found it." I was still drained, but I squeezed her hand. "But listen; are you sure you want this?" I nodded and she clasped her other hand around mine.

"It needs to be done, babe."

She nodded in agreement. "I know, I just don't want to lose you." She brushed my hair with her hand and gently kissed me on the lips. "Kes!"

He came stomping in with a large gun clutched close to

110

his chest. "Ma'am." He stopped in his tracks instantly while entering the room, snapped up straight.

"It's about time, Kes," she said to him. He walked over beside me and extended his arm for me to shake his hand, which I accepted, and he grasped my hand and bumped me on the back like in a 'bro hug', which was the first time I'd ever seen him not have a stick up his arse.

"It's been a pleasure, Miss Dyson," he said before turning to Ludo. "I'll pack," and then he ran off.

Ludo kissed me on the forehead as one single tear rolled down her cheek. "You are an absolute hero and it's been an honour to spend these last few years working with you and loving you; I have been very lucky."

I put my hand on her cheek. "Ludo…" she pouted at me, trying to stop herself from crying, "I love you too; thank you for saving me and so many others – it's time now." She nodded.

"No time like the present," I mimicked in her voice.

She set up a syringe and turned to me. "One last one, you ready?" I squeezed her arm and she injected me. Gradually, my eyes began to close, and I felt my brain shutting down; my body felt heavy, and I couldn't move anymore.

Then, my eyes closed, for good.

THIRTY-ONE

Now, for my side of the agreement, the whole reason I asked for Ludo in the first place, the thing I'd been keeping from you.

If someone else found themselves in my position, they'd probably try to take over the world or gain fame and riches or hide it a lot better than I did, but me, I just wanted to die. I wanted it gone and over with. As they say, *what you always want most is what you know you can't have.* So instead, I devised a plan to find Dr Habnossen, but with everything that happened, I managed to get her to find me with the help of the media. She said that word had spread quickly and that Kes always kept his eye out for any mention of her name, so through that, they looked me up and she knew she needed to meet me. So that brought them to me.

When we met, I asked for her help; I asked her if she could put me in a coma. She said it'd take her a long while to come up with a concoction that was strong enough to keep me down but promised that she wouldn't give up. During the time I was underground with them, we came up with a plan to travel with my body to the biggest forest in the world and for them to walk/hike around six hundred miles towards the middle, with no map, and bury my body so that no one ever knew where exactly my body was buried. If it were ever leaked as to which forest I was in, it'd still be impossible for them to find me. This idea overtook the idea to sink it to the bottom of the deepest ocean, partly because I refused to spend any more time of my life underwater and because they'd more likely be met by a coastguard on the waters than someone in the forest, even if it were to be poetic putting an end to it all in the water. I really felt for them as it wouldn't be easy walking that far normally, let alone with a dead body; plus, without a map, there was a chance that they may not make it out, but I trusted Kes's installed sense of direction to lead them both out safely.

I hoped this plan would hold me down for good, for the rest of eternity, or at least until the end of existence. It meant no one could get their hands on me and try and use my condition to their benefit for evil means, and it also meant that I didn't need to suffer anymore, which was funny to say when I had finally found happiness, my purpose and place near the end. I would've loved to have stayed and spent the rest of my life with Ludo and continued to try and cure everything that ever threatened people's health, but the sooner I was gone, the safer for everyone. Ludo and Kes managed to keep hidden years before meeting me, but I didn't think they were as much a priority to catch as I was, so it was only a matter of time before I was tracked down.

So finally, I was at peace and in my own way laid to rest, never to be found or used or to suffer again.

And then I woke up.

THIRTY-TWO

I woke up; *I woke up*. Why the fuck was I awake? How could this be happening? I thought our plan was perfect.

I couldn't hear anything. I struggled to open my eyes. I felt like my arms were floating but my feet were anchored to the ground. Not only had I inexplicably woken up, but I had woken up standing. My stomach felt woozy; I clutched my arms around myself. I could vaguely hear something in the distance. I managed to open my eyes, which were stinging and blurred. The white light made my eyes ping. My eyes never fully adjusted, but when I could focus a little more, I recognised where I was: I was standing at the grainy bottom of the sea, my feet cuffed solid into the ground and my arms moving like waves.

I should be scared, but I felt calm, at one. I didn't have to run because I was stuck, and no one would find me as I was lost.

Maybe this was my peace, trapped emotionless in my nightmare, my worst moment and alone.

AUTHOR BIO

CEON is Scottish. Based in England. They are twenty-three years of age. Queer identifying. Vegan living. This is their first novel, and they plan on writing and releasing more in the future. CEON writes a mixture of genres as well as taking part in other creative projects. You can find them on Instagram under: @cee_ceon. They want most of their writings to include LGBTQIA+ issues and mental health awareness.

 Matador

For exclusive discounts on Matador titles,
sign up to our occasional newsletter at
troubador.co.uk/bookshop